Would the icy wilderness that had brought them together separate Julie and Sam forever?

"Dear God," Julie breathed as the wind assaulted her face, "please help me find Sam, and please let him be alive and safe."

Cold numbed Julie's face as she struggled to fix her parka hood....Should she take the time to get her brother and father's help? As Kodiak picked up the pace, Julie decided against any detours. A delay could mean death.

The trail was overblown with snow. Steep, icy embankments lined the Bering side, and darkness made it impossible to see. But Julie was sure of her dogs and pressed on.

After an hour, Kodiak began to yip and slow his pace. Suddenly, the dog howled and danced around. Julie stopped the team and buried the snow hook.

"Sam! Sam!" she called out and listened in the silence for a reply.

Kodiak sat at the side of the embankment and whined. Julie grabbed one of the sled's lanterns and peered over the edge. At the bottom of the embankment rested Sam's overturned sled....

Julie was stunned....Her heart beat faster as she righted the sled, praying that it wouldn't reveal Sam's dead body. The sled turned over with a thud and exposed nothing more than an indentation in the snow.

"Sam, where are you!" Julie called into the night. The yips of several dogs sent her in search of their source. A few yards away, Julie found the rest of the team faithfully surrounding Sam's lifeless form.

JANELLE JAMISON is the pen name for Tracie Peterson, a freelance writer and regular columnist for a Christian newspaper in Topeka, Kansas.

Books by Janelle Jamison

HEARTSONG PRESENTS

HP19—A Place to Belong
HP40—Perfect Love
HP47—Tender Journeys

The Alaska Trilogy
 # 1

A Light
in the Window

Janelle Jamison

Heartsong Presents

*Dedicated to my good friend Pamela
Thibault who first interested me in the
wonders of Alaska and whose constant
faith in God and friendship has pulled
me through many rough roads.*

ISBN 1-55748-450-3

A LIGHT IN THE WINDOW

PRINTED IN THE U.S.A.

one

Julie Eriksson hastily donned her fur-trimmed cloak and made her way to the viewing deck of the SS *Victoria*. She strained to see the hazy blue outline of land. Nome, Alaska! After five long years, she was finally coming home. For the rest of her life, she would celebrate the seventh of October.

Squinting against the brilliance of the sun as it hit the ice floes in the Nome roadstead, Julie thrilled at the crisp, cold wind on her face. Where other passengers— visitors to her far north—shuddered at the zero degree weather and went quickly below, Julie felt like casting off her cloak. This was her home, and never again would she leave it. She longed to soak it all up.

The deep blast of the steamer's whistle startled Julie. She remembered back to 1919 when she'd left Nome for Seattle in order to study nursing. Then, the ship's whistle had been a lonely reminder that Julie was leaving home. Now an experienced public health nurse, Julie was returning to her people to offer what skills she'd learned in order to better their lives.

Her only regret was that her mother, Agneta, had passed away while Julie was in school. Having been a sickly woman, Agneta was Julie's biggest reason for becoming a nurse. What little health care existed in Alaska was inadequate to deal with the ailments of Agneta Eriksson. Julie had always desired to bring her mother relief from her torturous bouts with asthma. Julie had learned all she could about the illness, but she hadn't returned in time to help.

Her mother's memory would live on in Julie's heart, but the empty place Agneta's death left would never be filled. With this thought in mind, Julie wondered if her father and brother would be meeting her. Their homestead was some twelve miles northeast of Nome—a short, easy trip by dog sled.

She smiled as she thought of the dogs. It had been so long since she'd mushed her own team. City people in Seattle had laughed at her talk of mushing dogs, unable to image Julie handling the demand.

Of course, some of the rural students had known only too well the love of mushing dogs, and when several had invited Julie to join them at a local winter race, she'd readily accepted. Those simple kindnesses had helped ease her homesick heart that first year.

Glancing at her watch, Julie noted that it was ten minutes till twelve. They'd made excellent time with perfect weather for their six-day journey from Seattle. During her bleakest moments in the States, it had been hard to believe that Nome was only six days away. Most of the time the distance had seemed an eternity, and had

Julie not been resolved to become a nurse, she would have gladly taken the short trip home and forgotten the loneliness that haunted her in the state of Washington.

Julie felt the ship slow as the ice floes grew larger and threatened to halt the *Victoria*'s progress. Nicknamed the Grand Old Lady, the SS *Victoria* was one of the only ships to brave the harbor of Nome this late in the year. Julie knew that even the *Victoria* wouldn't challenge the icy waters past the first of November. Insurance premiums would soar due to the risk of icebergs. In fact, after the *Victoria* pulled out of the harbor for Seattle, there wouldn't be another ship into Nome until April.

"All for Nome! All for Nome!" a man called out through a megaphone.

Julie moved toward the man. "Are we going to take the ferry across the roadstead?" she asked as the man moved passed her.

"No, ma'am," the man said with a tip of his cap. "The ice is too thick. We're going to walk you across."

Julie nodded. It wasn't unusual for Nome-bound ships to anchor in the ice-laden harbor while passengers walked ashore across the thick ice. Leaning against the icy railing, Julie smiled to herself. Another hour and she'd be on the sandy banks of Nome.

"Oh, thank You, Father," she whispered in prayer. "I'm so happy to be home and so happy to be doing Your work." Julie glanced around to make certain no one was watching her before she continued. No sense in folks thinking she was daft.

"Dear God, make me an ambassador of Your love and good will. Let me help the people in this territory both with my nursing skills and my knowledge of You. And Lord, thank You so very much for allowing the years away to pass quickly and for the good friends You sent my way—friends who helped to ease my burden of loneliness and separation. Amen."

The ship came to a full stop, resting gracefully against the solid platform of ice. Julie raced back to her cabin and gathered her things. It was going to be a glorious day!

The walk across the icy harbor made Julie glad she'd bought a sturdy pair of boots in Seattle before leaving for home. Of course they weren't as warm as native wolf-skin boots with moose-hide bottoms, but they got her across the ice without any mishaps.

Some of the "cheechakos," the Alaskan name for greenhorns, were trying to snowshoe or skate in city boots across the ice. If she hadn't worried about hurting their pride, Julie might have laughed out loud in amusement. The only other women on the trip were a pair of frail-looking things who insisted on being pushed across the ice in sled baskets.

Julie wondered about the handful of passengers. Always there were those who came to find their fortunes in gold, but they usually arrived in April or May and departed before the temperatures dropped below zero.

There weren't many from the lower forty-eight who, upon hearing of days, even weeks, spent at fifty degrees below zero, would brave the Alaskan winter. Those hearty souls who did usually came for reasons other than acquiring gold.

Of course, some people were running from the law. Alaska provided a good place for criminals to escape from those who might put them behind bars. Others might have family or friends who'd beckoned them north.

Julie surmised the two women in the sled baskets might be mail-order brides. They weren't familiar faces, nor did they appear to be saloon girls. She felt sorry for them as she watched them shivering against the cold. She wondered if they'd ever bear up and become sourdoughs, as those who made it through at least one Alaskan winter were called.

Nearly losing her footing, Julie decided to forget about the other passengers. She was nearly a visitor herself, and she hastened to remember the little things she'd forgotten while enjoying the conveniences in Seattle. She kept her eyes to the ice, determined to keep her suitcases balanced and firmly gripped in her ladylike, gloved hands. *Useless things, city gloves,* Julie thought. She'd be only too happy to trade them in for a warm pair of fur gloves or mittens.

Not that it hasn't been fun to play the part of the grand lady. Given that Nome streets in winter were always in some state of mud, ice, or snow, Julie knew it would be wise to forget about dressing up. *No,* she reasoned, *sealskin pants, mukluks, heavy fur parkas, and wool scarves will be more comfort to me here.*

The wind whipped across her face and pulled at her carefully pinned black hair. Having spent most of her time indoors in Seattle, Julie's pale skin made an impressive contrast to her ebony hair and eyes.

Julie had her Eskimo grandmother to thank for the rich dark color of her eyes and shining hair. Having left her Inupiat Eskimo village, Julie's grandmother had married a Swedish fur trapper and moved to Nome. Their only child, Lavern Eriksson, had been born in 1865, some thirty-six years before the famed 97-ounce gold nugget was taken out of Anvil Creek near Nome.

It was the rumor of gold as early as 1899 that had brought Agneta's family north. While others were eager to make their fortunes, Julie's parents had found a fortune in love. Agneta and Vern had married after a brief courtship and soon Julie's brother, August, had been born. In 1902, Julie's birth had completed the family.

Julie scanned the banks again for a familiar face. She was about to give up hope when her brother's face came into view. His hand shielded his eyes, but Julie easily recognized his easy-going looks.

"August!" she shouted across the ice as she picked up her pace. Her brother pushed through the crowd and rushed across the frozen harbor to greet Julie.

"I can't believe you're finally here," August said as he pulled Julie into his muscular arms.

"Me, either," Julie said as she enjoyed the first hug she'd had in five years. She'd nearly forgotten the feel of supportive arms.

"Here," August said as he took hold of her bags. "Let me carry those. I suppose the rest will be brought ashore some time later?"

"Actually the *Victoria* is unloading immediately. The ice is much worse than they expected, and they want to get on their way."

"Great," August said as they came onto firm land. He put the bags down and asked, "Did you bring much back from the States?"

"Well, there are quite a few supplies for Dr. Welch and of course the things you and Father requested. Not to mention the dozen or more things that friends wired me to bring back from Seattle. I'd say maybe eight or nine crates," Julie said with a grin.

"That many?" August questioned as his eyes grew wide. "It's a good thing I brought a twelve-dog team."

"You needn't worry," Julie said as she linked her arm through August's. "At least half the crates are for Dr. Welch. They're marked with bright red crosses, so we won't have to spend time figuring out which is which."

"What a relief," August said with a laugh. "Look, you wait here, and I'll go get the dogs." Julie nodded and watched as August walked through the bustling crowd of people. It was good to be home.

An hour later, Julie was helping August load the last of Dr. Welch's supplies into the sled.

"I'll come back for our things after we drop these off at the doc's. Do you want to drive the sled?" August asked.

"No, you go ahead. I'm just going to walk and enjoy being back," Julie replied.

"Whatever you want," August said and took to the sled. "Let's go. Mush!" he called, and the dogs set out as if the sled basket were empty. They were a hearty, powerful breed of animal, well suited to the work and cold.

Julie trekked behind August, familiarizing herself with the few shops. The post office bustled with activity as the postmaster unloaded the incoming mail. Nome hadn't changed that much during her five-year absence. The Northwestern Commercial Company remained with a number of buildings that lined the main street of town, and folks could still get a meal at the Union Restaurant for four bits.

Up ahead, August had brought the dogs to a halt outside the twenty-five-bed hospital. Julie joined him just as Dr. Welch popped his head out the door.

"You're certainly a welcome sight," Dr. Welch said as he opened the door wide to receive August and Julie. "Let me grab my coat and I'll give you a hand."

August waved him off. "That's all right, Doc. I can handle it."

"In that case," Dr. Welch said with a shiver, "I'll speak with your sister while you unload the sled. You can bring everything around back. I'll have Nurse Seville show you where to put things."

August nodded and drove the dogs to the back of the hospital.

Julie followed the middle-aged man up the stairs and into his office. "I was able to obtain almost all the things you needed from the hospital in Seattle."

"That's a relief," Dr. Welch replied as he offered Julie a chair. "How was your trip?"

"Perfect," Julie answered and took a seat. "Of course, the destination alone made it that. I wouldn't have noticed if they'd stuck me in the galley washing dishes. I was coming home, and that made everything else unimportant."

Dr. Welch smiled and nodded. "I can well understand. Would you like something hot to drink?"

"No, I'm fine," Julie replied as she pulled off her gloves. "As soon as August finishes unloading the sled, we'll need to be on our way home."

"I'm afraid I must insist that you stay at least a day. Preferably two. As this area's public health nurse, you will report directly to me. Our combined reports will then go via mail to the proper officials. There's a great deal we'll need to cover before you can actually begin your work."

"I understand," Julie said thoughtfully, "but I have been working without much time to call my own. I need to go home and see my father, and I need time to rest."

"I confess, I haven't given much thought to your needs. Usually people go to Seattle for a vacation. It's odd to think of someone coming to Alaska for a break. I'm just so relieved to have an extra helping hand with the outlying population," Dr. Welch said as he took a seat across from Julie. "You will actually do many jobs that are often reserved for doctors in more populated regions. Especially as you venture out among the villages."

Julie nodded. "If August agrees," she stated as her brother walked into the room bringing a package, "we'll stay in Nome for one night. Then I really must take a short rest." Both Julie and Dr. Welch looked at August.

"There's no way I can stay. I'm needed to help with the dogs," August replied, reminding Julie of her father's sled dog kennel. "But I can leave part of the team for Julie to mush home tomorrow. I'll need to borrow another sled, however."

"There's one here standing ready for Nurse Eriksson's use," Dr. Welch offered. Julie smiled to herself. It was the first time anyone in Nome had referred to her as a nurse.

"Well, Julie?" August looked at his sister and waited

for her approval.

Julie nodded. "I think I can remember the way home," she said with a laugh.

"If you don't," August grinned, "the dogs sure will. Especially if it's close to dinner time."

"It's agreed then," Dr. Welch said. "Julie, you are welcome to sleep in the back room. There's a stove and plenty of coal. It's well protected from the wind and shouldn't get too cold."

"Once you get past 20 degrees below zero, it's just about the same. Cold is cold," Julie said like a true Alaskan.

Turning to August, Dr. Welch gave him instructions on where he could leave Julie's dogs and sled gear. "Oh, here. I almost forgot," August said as he handed Julie the package he'd been holding. "These are the things you asked me to bring. I was going to have you change before the trip home."

"You remembered!" Julie said with a note of excitement in her voice. "My sealskin pants and parka!"

August smiled as he secured his parka hood. "I'll tell Pa you'll be home tomorrow. Now if you'll both excuse me, I'll finish unloading the sled and be on my way."

Julie put the package aside and threw herself into August's arms. "Thank you, August. Please tell Pa I love him and I can't wait to see him again." August gave Julie a tight squeeze and was gone.

Loneliness seeped into her heart, reminding Julie once again of the isolation she'd known in Seattle. She tried to shake the feeling, convincing herself that because she was home, she'd no longer be lonely.

As she turned from the door, she could hear the dogs yipping outside, anxious to be on the trail. She understood their cries. She, too, longed to be making the trip home.

two

The next morning at breakfast, Julie couldn't contain her excitement. "I can't believe I'm finally home. I can hardly wait to see my father."

"I would've gotten about as much accomplished if I'd sent you on home with your brother. I suppose I should have realized the importance of your spending time with your family," Dr. Welch said as he and Julie accepted a stack of hotcakes from the Union Restaurant's waitress.

Julie laughed in animated excitement. "I feel just like a little girl at Christmas," she said as she poured warmed corn syrup on her cakes.

"We still need to pick up a few things for your trip home," Dr. Welch reminded her.

"Umm," Julie nodded with her mouth full. Taking a drink of hot coffee, she added, "I appreciate the supplies you've already loaned me. I'll only need to pick up food for the dogs. It's always wise to keep your transportation well cared for, just in case we get stuck on the trail."

"I heard tell a blizzard is due in," Dr. Welch said between bites. "I'm afraid you'll have to really move those dogs to get home before the storm catches up with you."

Julie glanced out the window. The skies were still

dark, making it impossible to get any bearing on the incoming storm. "I'd nearly forgotten about the darkness. How many hours of daylight can I count on this time of year?"

"I wouldn't expect more than seven—especially if that storm moves in as planned. The sun won't be up for another hour or so," Dr. Welch said, glancing at his pocket watch.

"I don't dare wait that long," Julie said thoughtfully. "I'll mush out in the dark. The dogs know the trail in their sleep, and I won't need more than two or three hours at the most, if the trail is clear."

"Are you sure you're up to it?" Dr. Welch questioned. "I don't intend to lose my first public health nurse. I've waited too long for help."

Julie smiled. "Don't worry about me," she reassured. "I've never been one to take unnecessary risks. I'll be fine if I can move out right away."

"Then I'll pay for this meal, and we'll go secure some food for your dogs," Dr. Welch said as he rose from the table.

Julie hurriedly forked the last of the hotcakes into her mouth and pulled on her parka. The warmth of the coat made her feel confident that she could face the trail without danger.

Julie affixed the dog harness to the sled, remembering to anchor the sled securely before attaching any of the dogs. Reaching for her lead dog, Dusty, Julie gave the strong, broad-chested malamute a hearty hug. "Good dog, Dusty. You remember me, don't you, boy?" she questioned as she led him to the harness.

Dusty yipped, and soon the rest of the dogs perked up and began dancing around as Julie talked to and petted each one. Within minutes, they were once again good friends.

After harnessing Dusty in the lead, Julie secured her swing dogs, Nugget and Bear. Two team dogs, Teddy and Tuffy, came next, with two wheel dogs, Cookie and Sandy, rounding out the sled team.

Julie checked the lines and then rechecked them. It had been at least five years since she'd had to be responsible for such a job, and she was self-conscious about doing it right. The wind picked up, reminding her of the expected snow.

"Well, boys," Julie said as she checked the ropes that held her sled load. "I think we'd best be on our way." She left the dogs long enough to go inside and bid Dr. Welch good-bye, promising to return in two weeks.

Taking her place at the sled, Julie paused for a moment of prayer. "Dear Lord, please watch over us and deliver me safely to my father and brother. Amen." She pulled up the snow hook and tossed it into the sled basket.

"All right, team. Mush!" she called, grabbing the bar tightly. She ran behind the sled for a few feet before taking her place on the runners. Soon she'd be home!

Once the dogs made their way out of Nome, they followed a trail that paralleled Norton Sound. Julie was relieved that, because the wind had been surprisingly calm through the night, the trail hadn't drifted much.

Julie barely felt the cold, even though the temperature had dropped to fifteen below. She was so well bundled beneath the layers of wool and fur that when snow started to fall, she barely noticed.

An hour later, the snow had worked into a blizzard with fierce winds blowing off the sea. Julie knew the dogs would stay to the trail unless something barred their way, so she moved on without concern.

The wind and ice pelted down ruthlessly, causing Julie to nearly lose control of the sled once or twice. The snow drifted and blew, almost obliterating the trail. Julie reassured herself by remembering that the dogs would be able to find their way through. Nonetheless, she found herself whispering a prayer. It wasn't until Dusty abruptly brought the team to a stop that Julie began to worry.

She couldn't call to the dogs above the blizzard's roar, and the blowing snow made it impossible to see up ahead. Julie wondered why Dusty felt it necessary to stop. She grabbed the snow hook and, after securely anchoring it in the ice-covered snow bank, made her way along the sled.

Taking hold of the harness, Julie made her way down the line past each dog. Finally coming to Dusty, she took hold of the tugline. "What is it, boy?" she questioned as she strained to see down the obscured trail.

Dusty whined and yipped but refused to move forward. Julie turned to move back down the line of dogs when someone grabbed her arm from behind. Her scream of surprise was lost in the muffling of scarves and blowing wind. She turned. A pair of ice-encrusted eyes stared at her.

For a moment Julie did nothing. Her pounding heart obscured all other sounds. She was surprised that the dogs remained relatively calm, and because even Dusty seemed at ease with this person, she began to relax.

The man let go of Julie's arm and motioned her to the sled. Julie nodded while the man took hold of Dusty's harness. Julie pulled the snow hook and grabbed onto the sled bar. The team barely moved as the stranger helped them down a steep embankment and across a solid sheet of ice.

The dogs couldn't get good footing against the slick surface, but the man moved them across with little difficulty. The snow let up just a bit, and Julie could see the stranger urging Dusty up the opposite bank. Whoever he was, Julie was grateful.

The dogs were struggling to get up the bank. Julie knew she should get off the sled and help push. She gingerly took one foot off and then the other. The ice offered no traction, and when Julie pushed forward, her feet went out from beneath her.

Smacking hard onto the ice, Julie lay still, struggling to draw a good breath. Tucking her legs up under her, Julie managed to get to her hands and knees. Just then she felt the firm grip of the man as his hands encircled her waist. Within moments, Julie was up on her feet and, thanks to the stranger, soon up the embankment.

Standing at the top to catch her breath, Julie thanked God for answering her prayers for safety by providing help from a stranger. She quickly resumed her place on the runner of her sled, ready to set out again.

The stranger moved forward. Julie could barely see the outline of another dog sled team. They would now progress together, Julie realized as the man waved her ahead. She felt much better traveling through the storm with a companion.

They progressed slowly, but evenly. Snow fell heavily at times, and the wind threatened to freeze Julie's eyes closed. Just as quickly, the wind would let up and visibility would improve. In spite of the questionable weather, Julie felt confident that nothing would hamper her trip home. She'd put the entire matter in God's hands, and she refused to take it back.

No sooner had this thought crossed her mind than the teams approached a river. Julie waited patiently while the stranger moved his dogs onto the ice. She watched silently as the man expertly maneuvered his animals across the river. It would only be a few more minutes before he'd signal her to start down the embankment.

Then the unthinkable happened. The stranger's lead dog disappeared into the river. Julie watched in horror as the stranger moved ahead of the team to pull his dog from the water. A sudden stillness in the wind carried the sound of cracking ice just before the stranger joined his dog in the water.

Julie had to act fast. She worked her dogs down the river bank and on a ledge of even ground. Fearful that the ice would give way and cause more harm, Julie tied a line around her waist and secured it to her anchored sled.

Cautiously, she worked her way across the slippery ice to the place where the stranger's dog team waited for their leader. The stranger was holding onto the edge of the ice, but it was impossible for him to get out. He'd cut the lead dog from the harness and was trying to boost him out of the water.

Julie reached down, took hold of the dog's thick, rough fur, and pulled him forward. The dog seemed fine as he found his footing and shook out his heavy coat. Untying the line from around her waist, Julie motioned the stranger to secure it under his arms.

Following the rope back to her own dogs, Julie took hold of Dusty's harness and pulled him forward down the bank of the river. "Forward! Mush!" Julie called against the wind. The dogs worked perfectly, pulling against the added weight of the stranger. Julie kept looking over her shoulder as she encouraged the dogs to pull. When she saw the man roll up onto the ice, she stopped the dogs and quickly crossed the ice to help the man to his feet.

Julie reached out her hand and helped the man stand. He seemed unharmed, yet Julie knew the possibility of hypothermia was great. She motioned to the man to take off his parka, but he shook his head and pointed up the embankment.

She reluctantly agreed to follow the man as he loaded his lead dog into the sled basket and led his dogs away from the broken ice. Julie retrieved her team and, feeling more confident of her abilities, mushed them up the river bank. At the top of the embankment, she could see why the man had motioned her on. A light flickered brightly in a cabin window.

With so much of the Alaskan winter months spent in darkness, all mushers looked for that welcoming beacon: a light in the window. Relief poured through Julie as she realized that shelter was so near. She moved her dogs forward and then realized that the cabin she was nearing was her own home. The dogs began to yip and howl as Julie mushed them on. They were home at last!

As Julie stopped in front of the cabin, two bundled forms made their way from one of the out buildings. Vern and August Eriksson both motioned Julie to the house while they worked together to care for her dogs.

August left Julie's dogs to his father's care and went to the stranger. He motioned him to follow Julie. The stranger pulled August to the sled basket and revealed his water-soaked dog. August nodded and pulled the dog into his arms. He moved quickly to the outbuilding where Julie knew her father kept the sick or weak dogs.

The stranger reached into the sled basket, pulled a canvas pack out, and made his way toward the house. Julie went ahead of him and opened the door. A warm wave of air hit her eyes as she walked into the cabin. Quickly, she made her way to the fireplace.

With no thought of the man behind her, Julie pulled off her heavy fur gloves and scarves. She pulled the parka over her head and tossed it to the floor. Thick black hair tumbled around her shoulders as Julie worked to loosen the laces of her mukluks. Kicking the heavy boots aside, she unfastened the catch on her sealskin pants and let them drop to the floor.

Beneath her sealskin pants, Julie wore heavy denim jeans. She felt them to see if they were wet. Finding her pants in good shape, she straightened up, brushing back the hair from her face. Staring at her from across the room was the stranger.

The shocked expression on the man's face nearly caused Julie to laugh out loud. Her black eyes danced with amusement, and a grin formed at the corner of her lips.

"I'm Julie Eriksson, and this is my home," she offered, extending her hand. She immediately liked his rugged looks.

The man broke into laughter as he took Julie's hand. "I'll be," he said, and his shocked expression changed to admiration. "I must say that's the first time a woman saved my life. I figured you were a man. I mean, well. . . ."

He fell silent as he dropped Julie's hand. "Of course," he murmured as he stepped back and allowed his eyes to travel the length of Julie's slim frame, "that's obviously not the case."

"I believe I owe you thanks as well," Julie said, growing uncomfortable under the stranger's scrutiny.

"I think we're more than even. By the way, I'm Sam Curtiss."

"Lucky Sam?" Julie questioned, remembering the nickname from things her brother had told her of his best friend.

"The very same," Sam said with a grin. "Although I think I owe my survival today to more than luck."

Julie nodded. "No doubt."

Sam shook his head. "So you're August's little sister," he said as he took a seat and kicked off his boots.

"I'm also a nurse," Julie said, taking a step forward. "And as such, I know that you're in danger of hypothermia. You should get out of those wet clothes and into something warm and dry."

Sam raised his eyebrows and crossed his arms against his chest. "Yes, ma'am," he said as he leaned back against the chair, "I'd say I owe this encounter to a great deal more than luck."

three

Sam refused to take his eyes off Julie while they waited for Vern and August to return from caring for the dogs. He was captivated by this woman as he'd never been by any other. She was so graceful and fluid in her motions, yet the knowledge that she had saved him out on the ice gave Sam a heartfelt respect for her.

As Julie moved about the room and tried to avoid his gaze, Sam's eyes lit up with amusement. She was uncomfortable in his presence—that much was obvious—and Sam wondered why.

Julie ignored Sam as she went about the cabin, reacquainting herself with the home she'd left so long ago. Vern and August, true to their Swedish ancestry, hadn't changed things except to add a portrait of Julie that she'd mailed them while at school in Seattle.

Julie circled the room, touching the things her mother had loved, cherishing the memory of days spent in her company. The house seemed empty without her. She grimaced as she remembered the day months earlier when the telegram had arrived. Because it was February, passage to Nome had been impossible.

Julie blamed herself for not being at her mother's side. Her schooling had been complete in time to return to

Nome before ice isolated it from the rest of the world. But because Julie had decided to become a public health nurse, there were certain additional requirements she had to meet.

When word reached her of her mother's death, Julie had had no other choice but to stay on at least until April when the ports reopened. By then, her mother's body would have long since been cared for, so Julie decided to finish her government training and return in the fall as a fully certified public health nurse.

Julie glanced up to find Sam's eyes fixed on her. His presence made her feel awkward. For the last few years, Julie had spent most of her time with women. Outside of the men she'd helped care for, Julie hadn't allowed herself the luxury of gentlemanly companionship.

The silence grew unbearable, but just as Julie began to fear she'd have to start talking with Sam, the front door burst open in a flurry of snow and fur.

"Father!" Julie ran across the room to embrace the elder Eriksson.

"Julie, it's so good to have you home. Let me look you over," Vern said as he put his daughter at arm's length. "You look more like your mother every day, God rest her soul. Of course, I see a bit of your Grandmother Eriksson as well."

"Oh, Father," Julie said with a smile, "come get warm by the fire. Here, let me help you with your parka."

"You're just like your mother. She was always fussing and worrying about me, even when she was. . . ." Her father's words trailed into silence.

Julie took the parka as her father pulled it over his head. "Even when she was dying?" Julie finished her father's words.

"Yes." Vern Eriksson seemed to age with the statement. "It hasn't been a year, and it seems forever. Wish it didn't have to be so for your homecoming."

"I thought I'd die for want of home," Julie stated evenly. Her voice strained slightly. "I'd rather it not be this way, but I've still got you and August." The young woman threw herself into her father's open arms. Her eyes grew misty.

"I see you brought Sam home with you," August said as he threw his coat aside.

"I think it was more the other way around," Julie said. "That blizzard hit hard, and I was still at least an hour from home. Sam appeared out of nowhere and, well, here we are."

Julie studied Sam for a moment. His brown eyes were so intense in their evaluation, however, that she quickly looked away.

"Don't you dare believe her," Sam's deep voice boomed out. "She saved my life. Pulled me out of the Nome River when the ice gave way."

"Are you all right, Sam?" Vern questioned with the voice of a concerned father.

"I'm just fine, Vern. Julie's quick thinking and my sealskin pants kept me from getting too wet. That daughter of yours is quite a dog driver. You ought to be proud of her."

"We are, to be sure," Vern said as he squeezed Julie's shoulders. "I'll bet you two could use something hot. Why don't you kick back, and August and I will get something on the stove."

"I'd like to unpack first," Julie said as she picked up her mukluks.

"Your things are already in your room," August offered. "I could pretty well figure out which crates were yours and which weren't."

"Thanks, August," Julie said as she walked over and kissed him on the cheek. "I could get used to being cared for," she said with a smile.

"Somebody as pretty as you ought to be cared for," Sam offered seriously. There was only the slightest hint of a smile on his lips. Julie blushed crimson, uncertain what she should say.

"Don't let her looks deceive you, Sam. She's wild enough to handle when she's got her steam up. I remember the time we were going to have to shoot one of the pups and—"

"I don't think Sam needs to hear about that," Julie interrupted as she shifted uncomfortably. She looked almost pleadingly at Sam, melting his heart and any protest he might have voiced.

"All right, all right," Vern said with a chuckle. "I guess anyone who's worked as hard as you have today deserves extra consideration. Go ahead and do what you need to. August and I will get lunch."

"Sam, you might as well put your things in my room. From the looks of the weather, you're going to be here tonight," August added.

Julie's head snapped up and turned to face Sam. *He's staying the night,* she thought as she met his laughing eyes.

A smile played at the corner of Sam's lips, and Julie was shocked to realize she was paying attention to them. It was even more shocking to wonder what it would be like to kiss those lips.

Julie lifted her gaze to Sam's eyes and found they had sobered considerably under her scrutiny. *What was he thinking? Did he know what she was thinking?* Julie blushed scarlet and dropped her eyes.

"I think I'd better get busy," she muttered and left the room. Why did he make her feel so strange? Julie chided herself for even caring. She was a nurse now, and her mother's dream for her was finally realized. There was no way Julie was going to jeopardize that dream by getting involved with a man. Even if the man was the handsome Lucky Sam Curtiss.

Julie marveled that her room hadn't changed in her absence. Her bed was still made up with the crazy quilt her mother had given her for her fourteenth birthday. Julie reached out and stroked the quilt as if it somehow allowed her to touch her mother.

"Remember, Julie," she could hear her mother say, "God only lends us to this world for a short time. What we do with that time, what we leave behind, is our representation of our love for Him. It doesn't matter that we make the most money or have the finest homes. What matters is that we can stand confidently before our Lord and King, knowing that we lived as He would have us live and gave Him our best."

This quilt was only a small part of what Agneta Eriksson had left behind, Julie realized. She'd lived her life for God and had brought both her children to an understanding of salvation. Surely God had welcome her as a faithful servant.

Julie sat down on the edge of the bed and sighed. She loved the simplicity of her room. A picture of Jesus praying, a small mirror, and a cross-stitched sampler were the only ornaments decorating the walls, while delicate, flower print curtains framed her window. A small desk and chair completed the room.

Julie stretched out on her bed and listened to the wind howling outside her window. The pulsating rhythm soon put her to sleep, leaving her to dream of penetrating brown eyes and a man she feared would change her destiny forever.

"Julie," Vern called softly as he gently shook his daughter. "Wake up. Dinner's on."

Julie wiped her eyes and sat up. "It's sure been a long time since I've had a wake up call like this."

Vern smiled and Julie noticed the wrinkles that lined his face and the gray in his beard. *When had he grown old?* she wondered.

"Come on. The food will be cold by the time you make

it to the table."

"I'll be right there," Julie said as she got up. "Just let me brush out my hair and change my shirt."

"All right, but it won't be easy to hold back August and Sam. They look mighty hungry," Vern said with a laugh.

"I'll hurry," Julie promised and went to her closet.

The clothes that hung there were those she'd left behind when she'd gone to Seattle. They seemed foreign to her. Finally settling on a navy print with long sleeves and a softly rounded, feminine collar, Julie dressed hastily and dug her hairbrush from her unpacked baggage.

Studying her reflection in the mirror, Julie thought she'd aged a great deal since leaving home. Maybe it was the trials of nursing duty or the loss of her mother, but she looked older than her twenty-two years.

She brushed back her dark hair and decided to let it fall just below her shoulders. There'd be plenty of time to pin it up when she was back at work. For now, Julie was determined to enjoy being a civilian without any obligation to a uniform or dress code.

She finished buttoning the cuffs on her sleeves as she made her way to the table. "Sorry to have kept you waiting," she said, taking her place.

"It was well worth it," Sam said with admiration in his eyes.

"Shall we say grace?" Vern asked and waited for everyone to bow their heads. "Father, we thank You for

Julie's safe return, and we praise You for bringing Sam and her through the storm. Thank You for the bounty You've placed before us. Bless this house and all who pass here. Amen."

Julie whispered, "Amen," and lifted her head.

Across the table, Sam lifted a plate of bread and handed it to Julie. When their eyes met, she swallowed uncomfortably and accepted the plate. Sam offered a broad grin before turning his attention to the reindeer steaks that Vern passed his way.

"So," Sam began the conversation while Vern and August occupied their mouths with food, "your brother tells me that you're about to embark on a new career. How soon will you have to report to work?"

"I, uh," Julie stammered trying to think of what to say. "I told Dr. Welch that I needed a rest. I've been working almost nonstop since I left Nome in order to study nursing."

"That's true, Sam," August said as he paused to take a drink. "My sister never does anything half-way. She completed her courses at the top of her class. She was suggested by none other than the hospital administrator for her position as a public health worker."

"I'm impressed," Sam replied with growing admiration.

It was exactly what Julie didn't want. She tried desperately to steer the conversation in another direction. "I know the need of the people in the villages. My mother was a good example. A doctor can only do so much. As a nurse, I can travel from village to village, and as a native, I'm already known to many and related to a great many more."

"Your mother would be proud," Julie's father said with a smile.

"I only wish I could have finished soon enough to help her." Regret darkened Julie's voice.

"Regret will only grow bitterness, Jewels," Vern said using his daughter's nickname.

Julie nodded. "I know. I'm not going to let it tarnish Mother's dream for me. I want to share more than medicine with the natives."

"Just what did you have in mind?" Sam questioned.

"Well," Julie began slowly as she put her fork down, "I would like to share the Gospel with them. Mother and I talked many times about caring for more than wounded bodies. We felt that there was a need to care for their wounded spirits, as well."

"Do you think folks in the villages will accept your ideas? They might not think too highly of a woman showing up to offer a cure for what ails them."

Sam's voice was lighthearted, but Julie resented his interference in her dreams. Instead of answering, she turned her attention back to the meal.

Vern realized Julie's silence was her way of dealing with things that hurt her. "I believe if the Lord lays a ministry upon your heart, He'll also open the necessary doors," he stated quietly. "Julie's felt this call for a long time. I have to believe that because she's gotten this far,

God has been in it from the start. She'll do just fine."

Julie flashed grateful eyes in her father's direction before allowing herself to look at Sam's face. She expected to find sarcastic laughing eyes staring back at her, but instead Sam's face seemed sober, almost apologetic.

The conversation took many turns after that, but Julie sensed that Sam wanted to say something more. When dinner was over, Julie insisted the men allow her to clean up the mess. She waited until all three had moved to the front room before she got up from the table.

The wind was still howling outside, and Julie knew without the benefit of an open window that the blizzard was raging. Part of her hated the long, dark winters when windows were boarded up to insulate against the cold, but another part of her loved the raw wildness of it. Days, even weeks, would pass when the only people she would see were those who shared a roof with her. This isolation was part of the region's attraction, and Julie knew she could never leave it for good.

"Still mad at me?"

Julie looked up from the dishes and met Sam's dark brown eyes. "I wasn't mad at you."

"Good," Sam replied, sounding relieved. "I'd hate for you to think lowly of me, especially when I think so highly of you." Julie's puzzled expression amused Sam. "You don't think a guy like me could think highly of a woman like you?"

"I don't know," Julie whispered. "I guess I never

thought about it."

"Too busy with your studies and all?"

"I suppose," Julie answered.

"Well then, it's about time you heard it from someone who cares enough to be honest with you," Sam said as he put his hand on Julie's shoulder.

Julie grew painfully aware of Sam's closeness. She had no experience with this. What should she do? Before she could do or say anything, however, Sam leaned down.

"I think I've looked for someone like you all of my life."

His breath was warm against Julie's ear causing her to shudder. She needed to move away from him, but in order to do so, she'd have to turn and face him. Making her decision, Julie turned quickly and found herself in Sam's arms.

"Don't. I mean, I . . .," Julie stammered. Why couldn't she say what she wanted to say? Then again, what was it she wanted to say?

"Don't be afraid of me," Sam whispered as he lifted Julie's face to meet his. "I'd never hurt you, Julie."

Julie felt her breath quicken at the sound of her name on Sam's lips. She could feel her heart in her throat. "I know," Julie managed to whisper just before Sam lowered his lips to hers.

The kiss lasted only a moment, but when Sam pulled away, Julie realized she'd wrapped her arms around his neck. Frozen in the shock of what she'd done, Julie met

Sam's surprised stare.

"Sam," August's voice called out from the front room, "we've got the chess board set up. If you're going to play, you'd best get in here."

The tension was broken by the sound of her brother's voice, and Julie quickly dropped her arms and moved around Sam. "I'd better get back to work," she said as she left the kitchen with Sam staring silently after her.

four

The raging wind and snow left Sam little doubt he'd be staying with the Eriksson's through another day. He smiled to himself as he dressed for breakfast. Julie would be there! He could hear her now as she moved around in the room next to his.

Maybe he'd been away from women too long, or maybe he'd been too selfish as a young man to notice, but the existence of a woman like Julie Eriksson was a welcome surprise to him.

Julie beat Sam to the kitchen where Vern had already stoked the fire in the stove. August had another fire burning brightly in the front room and several oil lamps had been strategically placed to offer the maximum light.

Julie knew better than to open the door, although a look outside was exactly what she desired most. She could hear the wind and knew the storm hadn't let up. How much snow would this blizzard leave behind? Two, maybe three feet? Julie thought of her upcoming job and wondered how much difficulty she'd have maneuvering the snow-packed trails. Maybe she'd grown too soft for the demands of her duties.

"Good morning," Vern said as he came in from one of the back rooms. "How did you sleep?"

"I was nearly asleep before I finished undressing," Julie said with a laugh. "I was just thinking that maybe I'm not cut out for life in the wilds after five years of civilization."

"Nonsense!" Vern exclaimed. "You have Eskimo and Swedish blood in your veins. That combination will overcome any obstacle in your way. You can do it, Jewels. I have confidence in you."

"So do I," Sam said as he stood leaning against the frame of the door. "I think you're more than able to meet any challenge. Of course, you'll find one or two unexpected surprises along the way, but you're one tough gal. I pity the obstacle that stands in your way."

"That's for sure," Vern chuckled as he motioned Julie and Sam to the front room. "Breakfast will be ready in a little while. You two relax in front of the fire ,and I'll call you when it's time."

"I wouldn't dream of it," Julie protested.

Her father wouldn't have any part of it. "I'm still in charge here," Vern said in mock sternness. "Now scoot."

Julie shrugged her shoulders and made her way to the front room. Plopping down on the sofa, she stretched her feet out to absorb the warmth of the fire. Flames snapped and crackled as the logs shifted in the grate.

"You make quite the perfect picture sitting there," Sam said as he took a seat at the opposite end of the couch.

Julie felt the full impact of Sam's stare and without

looking at him she replied, "I wish you wouldn't talk like that."

"Why?"

"Because I'm already humiliated enough. You aren't helping matters one bit," she answered simply.

"Humiliated? Why are you humiliated?" Sam asked as he leaned toward Julie.

She grimaced. "I don't know how you can ask that. I'm totally ashamed of the way I acted last night."

"You mean when August beat you at chess?" Sam teased. Julie couldn't hold back her smile. "That's better," Sam added.

"What is?" Julie asked innocently.

"The smile. I love it when you smile," Sam said softly.

Julie shook her head. "I don't understand you, and I don't know how to deal with you," she said honestly.

"Go on," Sam urged.

"Go on?" Julie questioned as she finally looked Sam in the eye. "What do you expect me to say?"

"I expect you to face up to your feelings. You don't have any reason to feel embarrassment. Especially not on account of our kiss."

Julie put her face in her hands and moaned. "I can't believe I'm sitting here talking to you about it. I get kissed for the first time. . . ."

"The first time, eh?" Sam questioned with a teasing grin. "So I was the first man to kiss you. I think I like that."

Julie groaned. "Let's just forget it. Please!"

"I don't intend to forget it," Sam said firmly.

"Don't intend to forget what?" August asked as he bounded into the room.

Julie fell back against the couch and rolled her eyes. Sam only laughed. "I don't intend to forget that your sister saved my life. I'd like to do something nice for her. Something special."

"You've already done plenty," Julie said as she got to her feet.

Knowing that August couldn't see him, Sam made a face nearly causing Julie to laugh. "I think I'll see if Pa needs any help," she said, struggling to keep a straight face.

Breakfast passed quickly with the men sharing all the news they could think of. Julie remained silent until the subject of the dogs came up.

"I'll need all the help I can get with the dogs this morning," Vern said as he finished a huge bowl of oatmeal. "That storm's wreaking havoc with everything, and I've got to get treatment to the sick dogs and food to all of them."

"I'll be happy to help," Sam said, pushing his chair back from the table.

"Me, too," Julie agreed. "In fact, why don't I take care of the sick ones. That's my field of interest."

"That sounds great," Vern said and smacked his hands down on the table. He'd made that gesture often throughout Julie's childhood, and it always signaled that he was ready for action.

Julie hastily finished her oatmeal and got to her feet. "I'll be ready as soon as I get my coat and mukluks."

"Then the rest of us better get with it, or Julie will have everything done before we get out there," August added.

"Sounds good," Sam said and reached over for his own mukluks.

By the time Julie came back into the kitchen, the men were ready to go. Securing her parka, Julie followed her father and brother, with Sam bringing up the rear. When Vern opened the back door, gusty wind sent them all back a step, putting Julie squarely into Sam's arms. Despite Julie's push to break away, Sam's grip remained firm. Deciding not to take the action personally, Julie continued to follow her brother into the snow.

"You come with me, Julie. I'll show you what I need done," Vern yelled above the wind. Julie nodded and felt Sam release her as she moved away to go with her father. She watched as Sam went with August to where the dogs were kept behind the house.

Vern ushered Julie into the outbuilding. While it wasn't warm, the building provided welcome relief from the blowing snow.

"Here," Vern said as he pulled Julie to the medicine cabinet. "I keep all my concoctions and tonics in here. We're blessed to have only five dogs with any health problems. One is Sam's lead dog, Kodiak. He's getting a little extra care after the soaking he got in the Nome River. Other than that, he'll be fine and doesn't really need anything."

"Do you want me to feed him?" Julie asked.

"Yes," her father replied. "I've got a drum of dried fish over in the corner and a barrel of my own special blend for the sick dogs."

"What's wrong with the others?" Julie questioned as she pushed back her parka hood.

"Buster tangled with a trap. He's in the pen along the south wall. I had to put twenty-two stitches in his hind leg. That ought to be easy for you to take care of. The rest have a bowel infection. I have a list on the table of what I've been giving them and how much food they're getting."

"Sounds simple enough. I'll start with Buster."

"If you're all right with all of this, I'll go help the guys with the regular feeding and watering," Vern replied and opened the door. "It's mighty bad out there. If you come looking for us or want to help, be sure to tie a rope to the post outside and then to yourself."

"I will," Julie promised and turned to examine Buster as her father closed the door behind him.

Julie worked for nearly an hour with the sick dogs. She offered each one a tender hand and a soft, soothing voice. The dogs whined and licked at Julie's hands as she stroked their fur.

"You're a good bunch of dogs," Julie said as she dished out their food into individual tins. The dogs cocked their heads first to one side and then the other as if trying to understand what she was saying.

After giving each dog their ration of food and water, Julie pulled her hood up and dug her mittens out of her pocket. Kodiak yipped and whined for extra attention, and Julie couldn't resist the look on his black and white face.

Putting her mittens on the hard dirt floor, she knelt beside the happy dog. "You're just like your master," she said as she rubbed the dog rigorously. "What is it with you two?" Kodiak licked her hand and then, without warning, gave Julie a hearty lick across the lips.

"You are just like him!" Julie exclaimed and got to her feet. She wiped her face with the back of her parka sleeve, picked up her mittens, and went in search of her father.

The wind refused to subside. Standing beside the sick dog building, Julie couldn't see the house which stood less than twenty feet away. The snow mixed with pelting ice, and Julie winced as it stung her unprotected face.

Forgetting her father's warning about tying herself down, Julie felt her way along the building, knowing that the dogs were just to the north. She strained to listen for any sound of conversation or noise as the men worked with the dogs, but the howling wind blended every sound into one massive roar.

Julie felt her eyelids grow heavy with ice as she moved past the edge of the building and, with outstretched hands, walked in the direction of the dogs.

Taking ten gingerly placed steps, Julie again squinted her eyes against the ice and snow in order to get her bearings. She couldn't see anything but snow. She called out to her father and brother, but the wind drowned out her voice. Fear gripped her heart, and Julie scolded herself for being so helpless. Bolstering her courage, Julie pressed forward. The dogs had to be just within reach.

After struggling against the storm's pressing power for more than twenty minutes, Julie admitted to herself that she was lost. Angry with herself for not heeding her father's instructions, Julie began to pray.

"Lord, I know I've done the wrong thing in not listening to my father. Please forgive me and help me find my way out of this storm." Just then Julie thought she heard the yip of a dog and moved rapidly in the direction of the sound.

She pushed back her parka in order to better hear and instantly regretted the action. Pulling the hood back into place, Julie wandered aimlessly, searching for any kind of landmark that would distinguish her whereabouts.

Cold seeped into her bones, bringing excruciating pain to her legs. Julie regretted having not dressed more appropriately for the outdoors. She'd remembered her mukluks and parka, of course, but she hadn't thought to bring along her scarves or to wear sealskin pants. Now she was paying the price.

Desperation caused an aching lump to form in her throat, but Julie knew crying would only insure worse problems. A heavy gust of wind took her by surprise, knocking her into a snowbank. Sitting in the snow, Julie suddenly realized how tired she was. Her mind felt muddled from the strain.

"If I rest for a minute," Julie said, rubbing her mittens against her frozen face, "then I'll feel clearer headed and be able to go on." Something inside her warned Julie that this wasn't wise, but she couldn't fight the need to rest.

Looking up, Julie realized she was snow-blind. There was nothing to indicate that civilization was anywhere nearby. When she moved to shift her weight, Julie heard a crunching sound come from within her parka. Ice had formed on her back and chest from the sweat of her search.

An alarm went off in her mind. That crunching sound meant that she was freezing to death. "Yes," she thought aloud as she got to her feet. "This is the way you freeze. You have to keep moving, Julie. You can't rest, or you won't wake up! Oh, God, send someone to find me. Please God, rescue me before I die."

Stumbling in her blindness and pain, Julie fell against the trunk of a tree. She leaned against it for a moment, licked her lips, and forced her mind to focus on moving. "I don't want to die," she whispered over and over. "I want to live."

Julie wrapped her arms around the trunk and sank into the wet snow. *It isn't at all unpleasant,* she thought. *If a body has to die, freezing to death is at least a simple way to go.* She felt sleep come upon her; they called it "the white death." *Funny,* she thought, *they also call tuber-*

culosis *white death,* because of the thick, white sub-
stance that patients cough up from their lungs. Why had
she thought of that? It was strange that something so
insignificant to her life as TB should come to her mind
now. She'd never need to worry about such diseases
again. Not now that she was nearly dead.

"Good boy, Kodiak. You found her. Julie! Julie, wake
up." Sam's face floated only inches above hers. "Julie,
stand up. Walk with me." Sam was pulling her to her
feet.

Julie tried to concentrate on his words as Kodiak
whined at her knee. She even attempted to give him a
smile. "I'm glad you found me," Julie whispered. She
tried to walk, but stumbled and fell against Sam.

Sam easily lifted Julie into his arms and pulled his way
back to safety on the rope he'd secured around his waist.
Was he too late? There was no way to tell how long she'd
been sitting in the snow. Sam gritted his teeth and prayed
that she would live. *She has to live,* Sam thought as he
moved quickly to the house.

five

Julie heard the men rushing around her. She felt her father pulling off her parka, while Sam and August worked to unlace her mukluks. She was dazed and groggy from the cold, and only the pain in her feet reminded her that she'd come terribly close to freezing.

"We've got to get her warmed up," Sam said as he rubbed Julie's feet.

"I'll build up the fire and heat some rocks to put in bed with her," August offered. "We can pack them around her blankets."

"Let's get her to her room," Vern suggested.

"Lead the way," Sam replied as he got to his feet and lifted Julie before August or Vern could move.

Vern nodded and August went to the fireplace. Sam followed Julie's father, ever mindful of Julie's near lifeless body.

"Put her on the bed," Vern said as he pulled back the covers.

"We'd better get her out of these clothes," Sam said without any concern for the propriety of the situation. "They're still frozen, but when they thaw, she'll be soaked."

"You're right, of course," Vern answered with a

worried look on his face.

Sam was already unfastening Julie's belt as Vern prepared to pull the icy denim jeans from his daughter's half frozen frame.

Pulling off the pants, Vern leaned over and felt the heavy woolen long johns that Julie had wisely thought to wear.

"These are dry," he said with a sound of relief.

"That's good," Sam said and added, "but this shirt was sweat soaked. It was frozen solid, but it's already starting to melt. I'd suggest you get her a dry one. I'll leave the room so you can change her privately."

Vern nodded. "I'll take care of it now. You might want to help August."

Sam reluctantly left Julie's side. His brown eyes betrayed the concern in his heart. *Dear God,* he prayed silently, *You must save her!* Pausing at the door, Sam shook his head and took a death breath before adding, *Thy will be done.*

August was lining stones in the fireplace when Sam entered the front room.

"How is she?" August questioned anxiously. He glanced up and met Sam's worried expression. "Is she going to make it?"

"I don't know yet," Sam said as he handed rocks to August. "She's pretty cold and her pulse is real slow. I wish I had my duck down comforter. It's of little use to anyone back at my cabin."

"We've got a goose down mattress on Pa's bed,"

August said hopefully. "Could we make use of it?"

"We might be able to cut it open at one end and slide Julie inside," Sam replied in an eager tone. "Would your father mind?"

"Not if it's going to save Julie's life," August said, dusting his hands off as he got to his feet. "It belonged to my mother. It was her most beloved possession. She always said it was like sleeping on a cloud. She wouldn't even use it for every day. Come on," he motioned. "Let's go get it."

Sam helped August remove all the bedding, and together they pulled the mattress off the bed.

"I can manage this," Sam said as he hoisted the mattress on his back. "You get some of those rocks. Get the flattest ones and we'll put them under Julie. The rest we can put over and around her."

"That ought to warm her up," August said and went to retrieve the rocks from the fire.

Julie moaned, speaking in her delirium. "Tried to find the way," she whispered. "Papa!"

"I'm here ,darling," Vern said as he finished buttoning the dry flannel shirt he'd just clothed his daughter in. He patted Julie's arm and talked loudly to her.

"You can't sleep now, my Jewels. It's time to wake up. Come on, we're all waiting for you."

"Too tired," Julie whispered. "Let me sleep."

Just then Sam entered the room bringing the feather mattress.

"If you don't object, I'd like to cut this open and put

Julie inside. I think the goose down will warm her faster than the wool blankets."

"That's brilliant, Sam," Vern said as he pulled a knife from its sheath on his belt and handed it to him. "Be my guest."

Sam sliced the end of the mattress open just as August came in with a tray of warmed rocks.

"This is going to be a real team effort," Sam said as goose feathers puffed out of the open end of the mattress. "Vern, if you can hold this, I'll lift Julie while August arranges the rocks on her bed. After he's finished, we'll put the mattress on the rocks and put Julie inside it."

The father and son nodded. Sam went to Julie's bedside. She looked so pale and helpless. Her dark hair spread out around her, making her face seem unnaturally white.

Sam thought she looked beautiful, more beautiful than any other woman he'd known. He'd lost his heart to her and prayed that she'd live long enough for him to share a place in her heart.

Cradling Julie as though she were a child, Sam stepped back and let August and Vern work. It was only a matter of seconds before they were ready to put Julie inside the mattress. Together, they eased her down into the goose feathers.

"Now, August, how about some more of those rocks? We can pack them all around the sides and put some on top as well," Sam said as he pulled the mattress up to meet just under Julie's chin.

Julie murmured incoherent words as the men worked around her.

"I'll get some coffee on the stove and warm some cider. That way we can start getting her insides warmed up as well," Vern suggested. "Sam, would you mind staying with her?"

"You know I wouldn't. Go on. I'll be here, friend," Sam replied and Vern hurried from the room.

When Vern returned, he took turns with Sam and August forcing warm fluids into Julie's mouth. The passing hours filled the men with apprehension. Were they doing enough or had they forgotten something?

As warmth entered Julie's body, she felt as though the blood were thawing in her veins. Pain roused her to consciousness. When she opened her eyes, Sam's face stared back at her.

"Hello," Julie said nonchalantly.

Sam smiled broadly. "Hello, yourself. How do you feel?"

"Buried alive," Julie said as she tried to sit up.

"You stay put, Jewels," her father spoke authoritatively. "You nearly froze to death."

"I remember," Julie said as she fell back against the pillow.

"You gave us a bad scare, little sister," August said, leaning over the foot of Julie's bed. "I think you aged me ten years, and I'm positive you did the same to Sam."

"That's for sure," Sam laughed.

Julie shook her head at the three men.

"How long did it take for you to find me?" she asked.

"That depends on how long you were with the dogs," Sam answered.

"It couldn't have been much more than an hour. Maybe half again as much."

"Well, let's see." Vern figured in his head. "We started around nine. That would've made it ten or ten-thirty when you left the building. We didn't find that you were missing until noon. After that we took turns looking for you. Sam and Kodiak found you just after two."

"Kodiak?"

"That's right. When we weren't having any success finding you, we decided to get help from the dogs. Since you'd been working with Kodiak, we put him onto your scent, and he helped Sam locate you."

"Is he all right?" Julie questioned weakly.

"Who? Sam?" Vern teased.

"No, no. Kodiak. He didn't get too cold, did he?"

"You stop worrying about that dog. He's doing fine," Vern chided. "We need to know how you feel."

"I hurt," Julie answered honestly. "I suppose that's a good sign. I feel like I ought to be issuing a lot of thank you's." She looked at the three men who watched her so intently and added, "I thank God for all of you."

Vern's eyes grew misty. "Come on, August. Let's get some more rocks heated. Sam, you make sure she drinks more of this hot cider."

"I will," Sam promised as Vern and August disappeared out the door.

Julie looked at Sam. He hadn't shaved, and the shadow of stubble on his face only made him more handsome. "Thank you for saving me," she whispered.

"You've already thanked me," Sam stated as he helped her to drink the cider. "Several times."

"I did? When?"

"When I found you. When you were laying here muttering in your sleep. In fact," Sam said with a self-assured grin, "you said quite a few interesting things."

Julie swallowed hard to steady her nerves. "I did? Well, I imagin the cold affected my mind."

"Oh, I don't know about that," Sam said in a thoughtful way that made Julie wonder what she'd said.

"Just who are you, anyway?" she questioned, causing Sam to burst out laughing.

"What a question! You know full well who I am. Your brother and I have known each other for seven years."

"I know all that," Julie said as she stared at the ceiling to avoid losing herself in Sam's eyes. "I want to know, well, I want to know more."

Sam laughed. "All right. Where would you like me to begin?"

Julie's forehead furrowed slightly as she considered what she wanted to ask. "I suppose at the beginning," she finally answered. "Where were you born?"

"Sacramento, California, in 1889—although we weren't there long enough for the ink to dry on the Bible entry. My father was bent on finding gold. He was always late to everything, including the gold rush."

Julie laughed. "Unlike his son who seems to make a habit of arriving right on time."

"My father had big dreams. He was one of the reasons I came on up to Nome after my mother died," Sam answered.

"Is your father dead as well?"

Sam nodded. "He got into a fight over a claim. The man took a knife out and killed him then and there. They strung the killer up not twenty feet from where my father lay dead and hanged him. My mother was never the same after that. She was left with three children and had no idea how to support them. The miners were good to her, however. They took up a collection and gave her three hundred dollars."

"What happened after that?" Julie asked, fascinated with Sam's story.

"She moved us around. Sometimes she did laundry for other miners. Other times she'd cook and run a boarding house. When my sister married and moved off, I was thirteen and my younger sister was nine. Ma moved us to Seattle where talk of the gold rush to Nome and the Klondike was all I ever heard tell about. It got in my blood, and I promised myself that I'd one day make the trip to Nome and find the gold that had eluded my father."

"Sounds interesting," Julie said, "but why did it take you so long before you came to Nome?"

"I couldn't leave my mother and sister, and they didn't want any part of it. My mother was getting old, so I went to work. I did a little bit of everything, but finally stayed with the shipyard work. My sister married at sixteen and offered to take my mother back East with her, but Ma wanted to stay close to where my father was buried. She made me promise to bury her in California, so I stayed on."

"You never married?" Julie asked boldly.

"No," Sam said with a smile. "I never found the right woman. My mother died not long before my twenty-eighth birthday and right after I got her buried alongside my father, I boarded a ship for Nome and never looked back."

"It must have been lonely for you," Julie said thoughtfully. She knew how the loss of her own mother had left an unfillable hole in her heart.

"Yeah, I guess it was in some ways. Of course, I had the comfort of knowing she was saved. I'd see her again, and that made it a lot easier to deal with."

Julie's eyes opened wide. "So you're a Christian?"

Sam grinned. "Yes, I am."

"Tell me how you came to know God," Julie said as she shifted her weight.

August and Vern came in with a tray full of rocks. "Sam, you take the rocks from the bed, while we put these hot ones in their place," Vern said, using tongs to place hot rocks around Julie's covered feet.

August held the tray, while Vern positioned each

rock. Sam put the cooled rocks in a pile on the floor, and when he reached beneath Julie to retrieve the rocks which August had placed underneath her, the girl began to laugh.

"I thought this mattress was a little lumpy. Now I see that it was just that I was sleeping on rocks."

Sam bent over her and reached across to get the last of the stones. He gave Julie a wink and quickly handed the rocks to Vern.

"We'll warm up another batch, Sam. How are you doing, Jewels?" Vern asked as he put a hand to his daughter's forehead. "You feel much warmer. That's a good sign. Let's just hope you don't suffer from frost-bite."

"Please don't worry, Papa," Julie said and pulled her arm out from the mattress to touch her father's hand. Feathers flew everywhere, causing Julie to sneeze. It was only then that she realized they'd stuffed her inside the goose down mattress. "What a wonderful idea! Who thought to put me here?" she asked.

"It was Sam's idea," August replied. "Sam was determined to save your life, and he usually gets what he wants. They don't call him Lucky Sam for nothing."

"Lucky Sam," Julie echoed as she looked up and met Sam's eyes.

"That's right, and so's the part about getting what I want," Sam declared.

Vern and August laughed as they left the room, but Julie bit her lower lip and stared thoughtfully at the man who remained at her bedside.

Sam returned the look and then spoke. "Now, where was I? Oh, yeah, you were asking me how I came to know Christ. Well, my mother was saved; my sister, too. I always tagged along with them to church on Sunday, at least whenever I could. When I was seventeen, I took a job on a fishing boat. We were pretty far into the Pacific one day when a storm blew up and destroyed the ship. I was left clinging to a piece of the craft, while the storm tossed me back and forth.

"I began to pray like I'd never prayed before. I asked God to save me, and I didn't mean just my worthless hide. I prayed for redemption, and I prayed for deliverance. Some people come to God in a quiet way, but I came to Him in a flash of lightning on the stormy Pacific. Right after I asked Jesus into my heart, a wave came crashing down over my head, and I kind of figured I'd been forgiven, redeemed, and baptized all at once."

Julie laughed. "What happened next?" she questioned as she caught her breath.

"He saved me. The storm calmed just like the time in the Bible when Jesus stilled the waves. I was found by another fishing vessel about an hour later."

"How fascinating," Julie said with true admiration in her voice.

"Yeah, I guess you could say that," Sam said thoughtfully. "I'm just mighty glad God never gave up on me. He's been a powerfully good friend to have alongside all these years."

Julie liked the open way in which Sam talked about God. It was exactly the way she felt about Him. He was so much more than a figurehead, sitting out there somewhere in heaven. God was a good friend and a constant comfort. Julie felt her thoughts blending to include her admiration of Sam. Had God sent Sam into her life for more than friendship? Already he'd saved her life twice, and whenever she was with him, the aching loneliness she'd known for so many years was absent.

Julie grew suddenly distant, and Sam put his hand out to touch her face.

"Don't," Julie whispered. Instead of getting mad, as Julie had anticipated he would, Sam just shrugged his shoulders and got to his feet.

"I think I'll go find us something to eat," he said and left Julie to contemplate her conflicting emotions.

six

Julie recovered quickly from her brush with death. She hadn't suffered any permanent damage, although her pride was sorely bruised. The day after her ordeal, she felt good enough to be up and joined the men in the front room for games of chess and checkers.

"Sometimes," Vern began as he lit one of the oil lamps, "I think I'll be glad when they string electricity this far. Other times, I'm just as glad not to have it to mess with. When the wind picks up past twenty knots, the lines blow down anyway, and then you have to dig the lamps back out."

"Yeah," August agreed as he moved his bishop to threaten Sam's queen, "but staying at the hotel in Nome sure spoils a fellow."

"When did you stay at the hotel in Nome?" Julie asked curiously. "I can't imagine either one of you leaving the dogs long enough."

"It was something your mother wanted to do," Vern answered.

Julie looked up from the table. "Mother? She always seemed to enjoy it here. I never heard her mention a preference for life in Nome."

"Oh, she wasn't partial to Nome. It was just that she

61

knew we'd never lived in a place with electricity or telephone."

"Well, I'll be," Julie said as she shook her head. "I never would have thought it."

"I never would've thought an old sourdough like you would have forgotten how to take care of herself in the snow, either," Vern said as his eyes narrowed ever so slightly. "Julie, you can't be out there on the trail without paying attention to your surroundings."

"Nor to the survival skills that you've no doubt known all of your life," Sam added.

Julie felt as though she were a small child being taken to task. "I know I was foolish. I've readily admitted it, and I've even taken to reading some of Grandfather's books about surviving in the North," Julie said, alluding to books that her mother's father had brought with his family during the gold rush.

"Books can't teach you everything. Besides, you've lived it almost all your life. You need to sit back and pay attention for your own good," Vern said seriously, adding, "August and I will work on your memory."

Julie smiled and jumped three of her father's checkers. "Crown me."

The day passed pleasantly, and as long as they sat in her father and brother's company, Julie didn't feel uncomfortable around Sam. She even enjoyed hearing about his exploits. Sometimes his stories involved August, and Julie shook her head in disbelief.

"I'm amazed that August never brought you home

before I left for the outside," Julie stated, calling the lower forty-eight by the term used by most people in the northern territories. She remembered the five years she'd listened to people in Seattle call Alaska "the frozen north" or "Seward's icebox." Julie just called it "home" and longed for it with all her heart.

"And I suppose that's as much a reason as any," August was saying as Julie stared blankly into space.

"Uh, sorry," Julie said as she cleared her thoughts. "What were you saying?"

"You asked why Sam had never come home with me," August replied.

"And?" Julie questioned over Vern and Sam's chuckles.

"And, I told you. Sam was working a claim that took all of his energy. He didn't dare leave it unoccupied."

"Yeah," Sam agreed. "I was fortunate to have August's help. I don't think I left the claim for the first three years."

"Do you still work it?" Julie asked, suddenly realizing that she knew very little about Sam's current life.

"No," Sam replied as he put August in check. "I sold the claim to the Hammon Consolidated Gold Fields. Mr. Summers, the superintendent, came out to offer me an impressive amount of money for the claim. I'd already made plenty off the mine and was thinking of selling anyway. By the time we'd finished settling, I had more money in the bank than I'd ever need to use."

"You could've sent it to your sisters," Julie said

innocently.

Sam's brow wrinkled and behind his beard stubble, Julie could see him grit his teeth. "They're dead."

"Both of them?" she questioned.

"Yes," Sam replied sadly. "My youngest sister was killed in an accident, and my older sister died during the influenza epidemic."

"How awful," Julie replied.

"We lost an awful lot of folks up here as well," August said as he conceded defeat to Sam. "Especially the Eskimos and Indians. They can't stand up to some of the diseases that accompanied the white man north."

Sam nodded and began to reset the chess board. "I know. I remember reading in the *Nome Nugget* that the influenza epidemic left more than ninety-one flu orphans."

"That's true," Julie replied, remembering the awful time. "Poor things. Some of them are still quite young."

"It's always amazing who lives and who dies in a situation like that," Sam said, sitting back. "I always wonder what God's overall plan is when I see a family of youngsters left without their folks."

"Me, too," Julie agreed. "And I have a real hard time when children are the victims of sickness. I've had to nurse dying children," she added, remembering her days in the Seattle hospital. "I don't think I'll ever get used to it." Her words sobered the atmosphere considerably.

"Yet," Vern finally spoke, "we have to trust God's

wisdom. He always knows best. I know when your mother was dying, she kept reminding me of Job and how much he endured. 'Curse God and die,' Job's wife told him. Agneta used that example whenever I grumbled too much about the injustice of her condition. She loved to remember Job's patience and strength whenever her own gave way to the sickness. Her favorite verse was Job 13:15: 'Though he slay me, yet will I trust in him.' I admired her loyalty. It strengthened my faith."

"I can well imagine," Sam said with a thoughtful look toward Julie. "A woman of strong faith is one to be cherished. I don't think God intended for any man to live alone."

"You know," Vern said as Julie won the checkers game, "I believe the Bible says that two are better than one."

Sam nodded. "It sure does. It's in Ecclesiastes. 'Two are better than one; because they have a good reward for their labour.'"

"'For if they fall, the one will lift up his fellow: but woe to him that is alone when he falleth; for he hath not another to help him up,'" Julie recited the verse from somewhere in her memory.

Vern reached for his Bible and flipped through its pages to Ecclesiastes four. He continued reading from verse eleven. "'Again, if two lie together, then they have heat: but how can one be warm alone?'" Julie glanced up at Sam and found his eyes on her.

"That's true," August added. "I remember times

when the weather was like this, and Ma would put us all together in bed with you and her."

"I remember that, too," Julie said, forgetting about Sam's fixed stare. "I loved it. I always felt safe and warm. It was so hard to leave and go to Seattle. It was like you were all here together in one safe haven, and suddenly I was left out."

"You were never left out," August said with a smile. "Ma always remembered you in prayers, and Pa talked about you constantly."

Vern nodded and reached across to affectionately squeeze Julie's shoulder. "That's true. Even in Seattle, you were an important part of our family. Almost as if you were never separated from us."

"That's sure not how it felt in Washington," Julie responded. Forgetting about Sam and how he might perceive her, Julie continued. "I remember watching Nome disappear as we steamed to the south. I wanted to jump overboard and come home. I was so lonely. School left so little time for any kind of social life, and I didn't get to attend church regularly because of my hospital duties." Julie needed to say more, but it was difficult to continue, so she fell silent.

"Didn't you have any friends among the other students?" Vern asked.

Julie thought for a moment. "I suppose there were one or two whom I felt comfortable with. We studied together and often worked together, but it wasn't like having a real friend. I suppose that's my own fault, though. I didn't want to be close to anyone."

"Why was that?" Sam asked.

"I guess I was worried about having ties in Seattle. I didn't want anything to hamper my homecoming. I suppose I created my own prison."

"Oftentimes we do," Vern said as he closed his Bible. "Everyone is different, and how they handle their fears varies. I wish I could have saved you the loneliness."

"Truth is," Julie said without thinking, "I still feel empty at times. I have my faith in God and my family, but, well. . . ." She paused for a moment, "I don't know. I guess I'm just anxious to be at my job." Getting to her feet, Julie was just as anxious to drop the subject. "Now, if you'll all excuse me, tomorrow is October twelfth and that means it's August's birthday. I'm going to see what I can whip up in the kitchen."

August grinned. "I figured everybody would forget."

"Just why do you think I was mushing this way?" Sam said and laughed. "Besides, why do you think I let you win at chess yesterday?"

"Well, if it was a birthday present, you should have let me win today as well. I'm a bit humbled by the entire experience," August said as he got up, stretched, and looked at his watch. "I guess I'd better go check on the dogs."

"That'd be a good idea," Vern said. "Let's go."

"I'll lend you a hand," Sam offered.

"No." Vern waved him off. "Somebody has to keep an eye on her," he said pointing at Julie.

"Me?" Julie questioned as she pointed to herself. "I don't need a keeper. I'll be just fine. I promise to behave myself, and stay in the kitchen."

Vern smiled at his daughter. "I'd feel better if Sam kept an eye on you."

Julie rolled her eyes and shrugged her shoulders before she let the men go. *Who was going to keep an eye on Sam?* she wondered.

By the time the sun began to set, the weather had calmed, and the temperature had risen significantly. The silence left in the wake of the roaring wind was unsettling.

Julie bundled up against the cold and waved off her father's protests. "I'm just going outside to look things over. There's no wind, no snow, and I'd best get used to the elements. I have a job to report to in little over a week," she said more harshly than she'd intended.

Vern nodded. "I can't help worrying. I love you, Jewels."

Julie's expression softened as she reached out to put a reassuring hand on Vern's arm. "I love you too, Papa. Please don't worry. I was very foolish the other day. I realize my mistake, and I won't make it again."

Vern embraced his daughter momentarily and then opened the back door for her. "Have fun," he said. Julie knew it was his way of giving her his blessing and confidence.

Julie walked out into the darkness. She turned back and saw the cheery glow of light shining from the house.

Out on the nursing trail, there would only be the lighted windows of strangers to look forward to. Was she doing the right thing? Was she really cut out for the solitary existence her job required?

"You're mighty deep in thought," Sam said as he came from somewhere out of the blackness.

"I was just thinking about my work."

"Apprehensive?" Sam questioned.

Julie looked rather quizzically at Sam. "How did you know?"

"Just something I felt."

"Well," Julie continued before Sam could get personal. "I'm sure everyone has second thoughts. I'm just settling mine, that's all. How about you? What brings you out tonight?"

"I just bought two new dogs from your father. We staked them out with my team this afternoon, and I was checking up on them. They fit right in," Sam said as he moved closer to Julie. "I figure we'll leave sometime in the morning."

"Oh, so soon?" Julie questioned.

"Disappointed?" Sam asked with a grin.

Julie moved away from Sam and noticed the skies. "Look!"

Overhead, the sky filled with pulsating light. Green, pink, and white lights streaked the night blackness, and the heavens exploded with northern lights.

"The aurora," Sam said as he came to stand directly behind Julie.

"I'd nearly forgotten," Julie said. She felt a trembling in her body at the nearness of Sam.

For a long time neither Julie nor Sam said a word. They watched the dancing lights as the colors faded, then radiated and grew brilliant again. The stillness of the windless night made the cold easily tolerated, but Sam moved closer to block the chill from Julie's back.

Julie decided she had to deal with Sam. He wasn't going to go away, and even though he planned to leave the next morning, it was necessary to tell him exactly where she stood.

"Sam," Julie said as she turned to face him. She hadn't realized just how close he was. Sam reached out and quickly pulled Julie into his arms. "Wait just a minute," Julie protested. "You can't keep doing this."

"Oh, yes, I can, and I intend to do it often after we're married," Sam said, refusing to let Julie loose.

"Married? I'm not going to—" Her words fell into silence as Sam lowered his mouth to hers. Julie expected the same brief type of kiss Sam had given her in the kitchen, but instead his mouth was firmly fixed on hers in a deeply passionate kiss. Julie had set out to concentrate on not responding, but that was easily lost as Sam aroused feelings inside her that Julie had never known existed. Giving in, Julie allowed Sam to pull her tightly to his chest as her arms went around his neck.

When Sam pulled back, Julie felt herself gasp for air. "You'll never stop feeling lonely until you give in to your heart and marry me. Remember, two are better than one," Sam whispered.

"But, I prayed about working as a nurse. I know it's my destiny." Julie forced the words from her muddled mind.

"And you are mine," Sam said before silencing Julie's protests with his mouth.

seven

On the first day of November, Julie reported to Dr. Welch at the two-story Maynard-Columbus Hospital. The whitewashed clapboard building offered the most thorough medical help in northwestern Alaska and had seen more than its share of action.

After meeting with Dr. Welch for a few days, Julie's confidence returned. Dr. Welch was habitually happy. He was at his best when he was working in and around his patients, and his nurses enjoyed his vibrant love of life. Emily Morgan, training to take over as head nurse at the hospital, told Julie that it was Dr. Welch's devoted wife, Lula, who'd made the gray-haired doctor so content.

"You know," Emily said as she showed Julie to a small office, "she married him right after his internship in Los Angeles. She's worked alongside him for many years."

"Yes, I know," Julie said as she slipped out of her parka. "I'm quite familiar with both the doctor and his wife. I was born in Nome."

"I didn't know you were native to Alaska," Emily said. "Oh, by the way, this is Nurse Seville," she added as a rather plain looking woman came into the office.

"Glad to meet you," the woman said, extending her

hand. "I'm Bertha."

"It's nice to meet you as well," Julie said and shook the woman's hand. "I'm Julie Eriksson."

"Well, it's quite a challenge you've carved out for yourself. I've made calls with Dr. Welch to the nearest Eskimo settlements, and I've never really enjoyed the sled travel. Although I must say, Doc enjoys every bit of it. But you'll be out there on your own, driving your own team and facing the elements. I admire your spirit," Bertha said honestly.

"Thank you," Julie answered just as Dr. Welch entered the room.

"Are you ready to go?" he questioned as he took a seat behind a paper-laden desk.

"I sure am," Julie responded. "I came to say good-bye and see if there were any last-minute instructions."

"Take good care of your dogs," Welch answered firmly. "Of course, take good care of yourself as well. Keep good records, and let me know if there's anything that needs my attention."

"I will," Julie promised and picked up her parka. "I'd best be on my way. My first stop is nearly two hours away."

"At least the weather's been good. Unseasonably so, if you ask me," the veteran doctor replied. After nearly twenty years in Alaska, he spoke with authority.

"Well, remember me in your prayers," Julie said as she pulled on her coat.

"That we will," Nurse Emily replied.

Mushing out on the open trail, Julie had plenty of time to think. Too much time. She'd been working for nearly six weeks, and during that time, she'd seen just about everything.

She'd delivered babies, set broken bones, stitched up wounds, and dealt with a multitude of other ailments. Over all, her experience had been a good one, but always there were the hours alone on the trail when the only thing she could think about was Sam.

How could one man affect a woman so much that she questioned her purpose in life? Ever since Sam had kissed her and told her he intended to marry her, Julie had been confused.

When Julie was younger and there had been only her mother's driving desire to see her daughter become a nurse, she'd felt certain of her destiny. But Sam was just as strong in maintaining that Julie was his destiny.

Julie stopped the dogs for a brief rest. There were only three to fours hours of light a day as Christmas grew near. Usually she woke up in the darkness and mushed out, only to spend the daylight hours inside a sod igloo, delivering a baby or tending to some other medical need. She was enjoying this rare opportunity to travel during the daylight hours.

Julie checked her compass and pulled out a small map from inside her parka. If everything went according to plan, she'd be in the next village within two hours. Carefully replacing the compass and map, Julie checked her dogs and took her place at the back of the sled.

"Let's mush," she called out, and the dogs immediately picked up a nice trotting pace.

Julie alternated running behind the sled and riding the runners. She'd gradually regained her muscular arms and running legs. Physically, she'd never felt better, but emotionally, she was drained.

"God, please help me," she prayed. The winter sky's pale turquoise color was already giving way to the coming darkness. In the distance, Julie saw the tell-tale signs of a snow storm. She called to the dogs to pick up the pace before turning her mind and soul back to God in prayer. "Lord, I don't understand why You sent Sam into my life at this time. I thought I knew what You wanted me to do, but how can I do that and care for a husband? And if You don't want Sam to be my husband, then why did You allow him to complicate things for me?" Julie realized how selfish her prayer sounded and fell silent.

She watched the frozen wasteland pass by her moving sled. The horizon stretched out forever, and yet, just ahead Julie would thrill to the light in the window of some thoughtful villager, and once again she'd be safe.

The dogs seemed to sense the end of the journey and hastened to the place where they would receive fresh tom cod and tallow. *They are smarter than human beings,* Julie thought. *They never press on in a storm when they know it's dangerous, and they're content to do their work and take their rest. If only I could be the same.*

Blackness fell long before Julie reached the small Eskimo village. She kept watch through the darkness as the dogs, confident of their trail, pressed on.

Visions of Sam filled her mind, and for a moment Julie allowed herself to wonder what it would be like to marry Lucky Sam Curtiss.

"Surely I'd have to give up my nursing," Julie mused. "He would expect me to give him my undivided attention. And there would be the possibility of children. A man like Sam would probably want a dozen or more," she added sarcastically. "But then, I hope to one day have a big family, too.

"Why did he have to come?" Julie yelled into the darkness. She hadn't noticed that they were nearly upon the village, and only when Dusty brought the team to a stop did Julie realize why.

"Good boy, Dusty. I was daydreaming again," Julie said as she planted the snow hook.

A middle-aged Eskimo man appeared with his two sons. She recognized the man as George Nakoota. She had tended his youngest child during a bad bout of tonsillitis during her first visit to the village.

"There's warm food inside for you," George said as he helped Julie unload her sled. "The boys and I will take care of the dogs." Julie nodded and went inside. As long as the dogs were fed and bedded down, she could rest.

George's wife, Tanana, helped Julie out of her parka and mukluks. "George heard you coming from far off," Tanana said as she placed the parka over a chair by the oil can stove.

"I don't see how George can hear these things from so far away," Julie said. "He's always saying that he can hear any storm or animal coming for fifty miles. Those are mighty perceptive ears."

"George does not listen with his ears. He listens with his soul. George and the land are close, like old friends."

"The soul can tell a person a great deal, if we choose to listen to it," Julie agreed. "Have you thought about what I told you when I was here before?"

"I remember when your father used to visit with George and tell him about white man's God in Heaven. George said it made nights pass faster with stories from your Bible."

"But they're more than stories, Tanana." Julie hoped her old friend wouldn't be offended by her boldness. "I know you're skeptical of the things that white folks bring to your people—the sickness and disease, the mining operations and such—but honestly, Tanana, God has a great deal of love for you and your people."

"I know that," Tanana agreed, "but He loves me in the Eskimo way."

George came in bringing the rest of Julie's gear. "Your dogs are looking good, Julie. You've been taking good care of them."

"The people have all been so good to me," Julie said as she sat down at the small crude table where Tanana was dishing up hot food. "They feed the dogs and me and always give us a warm place to sleep. I have no complaints."

"Any trouble with animals?" George asked as he joined Julie at the table. "I noticed that Dusty looked a bit chewed on."

"He was," Julie nodded. "You've got eyes that are every bit as good as your ears, George. He got into a fight with a village dog. The other dog looks worse, so we count it a victory for him. I'd appreciate it if you didn't tell him otherwise."

George laughed. "You spoil him. He'll grow fat and lazy and never run fast, but I won't tell him."

Julie stayed on in George's village for two days. She treated several bad colds and looked in on George's mother who'd suffered from an infected wound on her hand. Julie was preparing to leave when George's oldest son came running.

"My father's been hurt," he said breathlessly as he pulled at Julie's arm.

"What happened?" Julie asked, pulling her medical bag from the sled.

"The dogs were fighting, and he tried to pull them apart. His arm is pretty bad."

Julie followed the boy on a dead run to the opposite side of the village where George had been carried to his house. When Julie walked into the house, George had already been placed on the small kitchen table. His arm was a bloody mangled mess, and Julie wasn't sure that she could save it.

She motioned George's son to hold a cloth to his

father's arm. "Put pressure here while I prepare my instruments. Tanana, I'll need some hot water. George, George, can you heard me?" Julie questioned as she leaned down.

"I hear you," George said between gritted teeth.

"I'm going to clean your arm and see what's what. I'm going to do a lot of stitching, and I'd just as soon you not have to be awake for it. I've got some chloroform, and I'm going to put you to sleep," Julie said as she prepared a place for her instruments.

"Julie," George whispered weakly.

He was losing a great deal of blood, and Julie knew she'd have to hurry. "What is it, George?"

"You gonna pray for me?"

"Of course," Julie said with a smile.

"Your pa has talked to me before," George paused and drew a deep breath before continuing, "about eternal life. I think I need to have that about now."

George was always good natured, even when he was bleeding to death, Julie decided. Nevertheless, she continued as if George had nothing more complicated than a splinter. "John 3:16 says, 'For God so loved the world, that he gave his only begotten Son, that whosoever believeth in him should not perish, but have everlasting life.' You must believe that God sent His Son to save your life. Do you believe that, George?" Julie asked as she washed her hands in carbolic acid before pouring a great amount into a bowl for her instruments.

"I believe," George whispered.

"Then pray with me, George," Julie said as she took fresh water from Tanana. "Dear Father, George knows he's a sinner, and he wants your forgiveness," Julie paused to wave George's son away and poured water over his father's arm.

George bit his lip, but refused to cry out. "I'm a sinner God. Forgive me," he said and looked up at Julie.

Julie nodded and continued, "George wants to accept Your Son, Jesus, so that he might have eternal life."

"I want eternal life," George murmured. "I want Your Son, Jesus."

"And, Lord," Julie said as she poured disinfectant over the mangled limb, "help me to mend George's arm. Amen."

George nodded, too weak to speak. Julie poured a liberal amount of chloroform on a clean cloth. "I'm going to put you to sleep now, George." She placed the cloth over George's nose and mouth.

Instantly, George was rendered unconscious, and Julie flew into action. She picked her way through the strips of flesh, cleaning each one thoroughly and moving on to the deep gashes.

Tanana held a lantern to one side. Periodically, Julie felt for George's pulse and respiration. He was doing well, and Julie felt confident that his relative good health and God's direction would see her through the situation.

After two hours, Julie stood back and assessed her work. Barring infection, George would retain full use of his arm. She decided to stay on in the village until she felt confident that the wounds were free from contamination.

Dragging her weary body to bed, Julie thanked God for His direction. She fell asleep listening to George's rhythmic breathing.

With George well on the way to recovering and Christmas only three days away, Julie readied once again to return to Nome. She was determined to be home for Christmas, but she hadn't managed to do any Christmas shopping yet.

She was rechecking the dog's harness when Tanana approached her. "You have my gratitude for saving George's life. I thanked your white God, too."

"He can be your God as well, Tanana," Julie said as she turned from the dogs.

Tanana nodded and held out several packages. "I'll think about your words, Nurse Julie. These are for you. They are payment for George. I know your Christmas is coming soon, and maybe you will need things for your father and brother. I have made two pairs of sealskin mukluks. They have fox fur inside to make them extra warm."

"Thank you, Tanana. I'll give them to my father and brother for Christmas and tell them that you made them."

The woman smiled broadly and backed up a step. "You are welcome here anytime. We'll look forward to seeing you after your celebration."

Julie nodded and rallied her team. "Mush!" she called out and held onto the sled handle as the dogs, eager to be on the trail, moved out.

Nome looked the same as when Julie had left. She knew she ought to go directly to Dr. Welch's office at the Merchants and Miners Bank of Alaska, but keeping in mind that it was Christmas Eve, she took time, instead, to do a bit of shopping.

She searched through several shops, looking for just the right gifts for Vern and August. She finally settled on some tools for her father and a guitar for August. She smiled as she brought the items out to her sled. August had always wanted to learn to play the guitar, and now Julie would hound him until he could play her a tune.

Julie wrapped the gifts safely inside a large fur pelt and loaded them onto the sled. She started to walk down the street to the hospital when something in the store window caught her attention. A handsome, ivory-handled knife was prominently displayed.

Julie went inside and asked to see it in order to better study the detail of the carving. A talented craftsman had skillfully transformed the ivory into an intricate piece of art. The outline of a dog driver with his sled team was highlighted on the handle of the knife.

Impulsively, Julie purchased the knife for Sam. She hadn't seen in him seven weeks, but the urge to buy him a Christmas gift overruled her better judgment.

Adding the knife to the other gifts on the sled, Julie went in search of Dr. Welch.

eight

Julie found Dr. Welch, and after quickly exchanging her paperwork and personal assessments of the villages she'd visited, she bid him a Merry Christmas and received permission to go home for the holidays.

"You know," Dr. Welch said as he followed Julie outside, "we're having a bit of a Christmas Eve party, and I know Lula would love for you to join us."

"I've never been one for parties," Julie answered honestly. "I'm just a home girl. I want to be with my family."

"I understand," Dr. Welch said with a smile. "You have a well-deserved rest, and I'll see you the day after New Year's."

"I'll be here," Julie replied with a wave.

Making her way to the dogs, Julie started thinking of Sam. Would he make an appearance on Christmas, and if he did, would she be happy to see him? She tried to forget about him and concentrate on getting home, but nothing could get him out of her thoughts.

Julie looked over each of her dogs, checking their paws and bellies for signs of freezing. They were tired and deserved a good rest, but Julie had no alternative but to mush them home.

"Your team looks a bit spent."

Julie smiled before straightening up to meet Sam's bearded face. "I'll give you that much," she said pushing her parka hood back. Her black hair had been neatly braided when she'd started out that morning, but now wisps of it blew around her face.

"Is that all?" Sam said with a grin. "I haven't seen you in nearly two months. I was beginning to think I'd scared you off. Thought I might have to come find you."

Julie put her hands on her hips. "Same old Sam."

Sam laughed and watched Julie as she finished with her dogs. "I've been thinking about you," he said. "Now that I know what it is to have you in my arms, I couldn't stop thinking about it."

Julie stiffened slightly. She was unprepared for Sam's boldness. How should she react? Nervously, she shifted from one foot to the other. "I certainly hope you don't plan to repeat the scene here in the middle of Nome's Front Street."

"Why not?" Sam said as he took a step toward Julie.

"Oh, no," Julie said, backing up. "You can't mean it. I have a reputation to preserve, if not for myself, for my career."

Sam stopped and shook his head. "I'm never going to do anything but honor and love you. I would throttle any man, or woman, for that matter, who might blemish your reputation. However, I think your dogs have earned a rest. Let's take them over to my cabin. I'll hitch my dogs, and we'll give yours a break. There's a snow building up, and I don't want you out here alone. I'll take you home."

"No," Julie protested. "My dogs will be fine. It's only another twelve miles. I couldn't ask you to—"

"You didn't ask, and I am telling you," Sam said as he pointed to the sled. "I expect you to get in the basket while I mush these dogs to my house. If you don't get in on your own, I'll put you there myself. Then we'll just see how your reputation withstands the talk."

"I will not," Julie said as she moved to the back of her sled. She thought to jump on the runners and order Dusty into action, but Sam outmaneuvered her and took hold of Dusty's tugline.

Sam raised a questioning eyebrow and waited for Julie to respond. Julie matched his stare. Her breathing quickened as a smile played at the corner of Sam's lips. He waved his hand in front of him and motioned Julie to the sled.

"All right," Julie said and carefully climbed into the sled basket, narrowly avoiding the gifts she'd purchased. "I give up. You win. Take me home."

Sam laughed and dropped the tugline. He walked down the side of the dog team and leaned over Julie. "That's a good girl," he said and dropped a kiss on her forehead.

Julie squirmed away, blushed, and pulled her hood back in place so that Sam couldn't see her face. She wondered who all in Nome had seen Sam's actions, but before she could glance around, Sam was moving the dogs out.

While Julie enjoyed the ride to Sam's house on the outskirts of Nome, she was also nervous. Just knowing that Sam stood on the runners behind her made Julie apprehensive. She tried to concentrate on the excitement of seeing her father and brother and celebrating Christmas.

When Sam stopped in front of the two-story clapboard house, Julie was impressed. It wasn't the type of place she'd pictured Sam in.

"We're home," Sam said in a jovial way. "One day I'll say that, and it'll be true."

Julie tried to appear unaffected by Sam's words, but when he reached down to help her from the basket, she nearly jumped out the opposite side of the sled.

"I wish you'd stop," she said and pushed back her parka hood to better see Sam. "I don't know why you insist on doing this, but I want to go home, and if you aren't going to behave, then I'll drive myself." She was determined to stand her ground.

"You're tired, Julie," Sam said ignoring her protest. "Why don't you go inside and make yourself comfortable?"

"I can wait out here," Julie said anxiously.

"I know you can wait out here. I know you can mush dogs through bitter cold and horrible blizzards. I know, too, that you have a mind of your own, but I'm every bit as stubborn, and I'm telling you to go in the house and warm up." Sam's words were stern, yet Julie knew they were given out of concern for her welfare.

"I'm touched that you care, Sam, but—"

In three long strides, Sam was at Julie's side. He hoisted her over his shoulder as if he were carrying a sack of grain.

"Put me down," Julie yelled and pounded against Sam's back.

"I'll put you down when we're in the house. We're wasting what few daylight hours we have because you can't cooperate," Sam said as he carried Julie into his house.

Once they were inside, Sam put Julie down. She expected him to try to kiss her again, so she moved quickly away. "All right, you've had your way," she said with a trembling voice.

"Not hardly," Sam said with a grin. "I haven't married you yet." He turned with a laugh and walked out the front door.

Once he was outside, Sam stopped laughing. He'd come very close to pulling Julie into his arms and was still trembling himself when he went to unharness the dogs.

He thought about what he'd done as he fed and watered Julie's team. Sam had never imagined that he'd see Julie in Nome. It had been his plan to question Dr. Welch about her schedule and surprise her for Christmas. But the surprise had been his when he found her standing on Front Street preparing to leave town.

Sam rubbed his beard and sighed. She was a beautiful woman, but more than that, she was intelligent and self-confident, although a bit too stubborn. She was exactly everything that he'd prayed for, everything and more.

"Thank You, God, for sending Julie into my life. I feel sure she's the one You would have me marry. I've prayed so long for a Christian wife, and if Julie is the right one, Lord, then I pray You will help her to see me as the man You have chosen for her. Above all else, Lord, protect her from harm. In Jesus' name, Amen."

Sam glanced back at the house. The woman he planned to marry was sitting inside the home he hoped to one day share with her. He would have loved nothing more than to go inside and share her company in the comfort of his home, but he knew it would only make Julie more uncomfortable, so he put the thought aside.

Sam finished harnessing his eager dogs to Julie's sled. He gave his lead dog, Kodiak, a brief pat on the head before going inside to retrieve Julie.

"You're anxious to be on the road, aren't you, boy?" Kodiak whined as though answering, and Sam laughed. "I'm going. I'm going. I just have to go get our girl, and we'll be off."

Sam bounded up the front steps and peered cautiously through the doorway in case Julie planned to throw anything at him. The sight that caught his eye caused Sam to stop in his tracks. Julie lay innocently sleeping on the couch.

Sam called her name, but Julie slept too deeply to hear him. He approached her sleeping form and gently stroked her cheek. It was rosy from the wind, but soft—just as he remembered from the time he'd last kissed her.

Avoiding the memory, Sam went outside and made a place in the basket for Julie. Once he'd placed several blankets in the basket, Sam went back inside. He threw several of his own things into a pack and loaded it onto the sled. Finally, Sam trudged through the snow to the house of his neighbor, Joe Morely, a bachelor who often traded favors with Sam.

Sam let Joe know he'd be gone for several days and asked if he'd mind tending the dogs. After receiving Joe's promise to watch over the house and animals, Sam went back to his house.

Julie slept soundly as Sam lifted her into his arms and carried her to the sled. The cold air caused her to stir and nestle her face against his chest, but she slept on, dreaming of warm arms and a man named Sam.

nine

Julie woke up just as Sam led the dog team down the embankment of the Nome River. She couldn't believe that he had packed her into the sled to sleep away the miles between Nome and the Eriksson homestead. Wiping sleep from her eyes, Julie worked her way out of the covers and sat up.

The sky was gray and heavy with snow. Julie knew it would only be a matter of time before those clouds would open up and dump another white blanketing on the Alaskan coastline.

"We're nearly there," Sam said as he moved out on the river ice.

"I hope we're not about to repeat scenes from our last shared trip across the Nome," Julie called up from the basket.

Sam laughed good naturedly. "You'd better mind your manners, or I'll make you get out and walk, and we both know your ability on ice is questionable."

Julie laughed. "I can manage."

"No doubt," Sam said as he reached the opposite bank. He jumped off the runners and pushed as his ten-dog team pulled. Within seconds they were over the top.

In the fading light, Julie could see the welcoming sight of her home. She would be home with her family for

Christmas. In the distance the dogs yipped and howled as Sam's team drew near, alerting Vern and August to their arriving visitors.

Sam halted the sled at the back door and helped Julie from the sled. "You go on in, and I'll unload the basket and take care of the dogs."

Julie started into the house but remembered her gifts. "I need to unpack some of it myself," she said as she turned back to the sled.

"I can take care of it," Sam insisted.

"Look, I'm not just being stubborn this time," an exasperated Julie tried to reason. "I have to take care of some of it myself. It is Christmas Eve, after all."

"I see," Sam said with a grin. "Anything for me?"

"That's a rather presumptuous question," Julie replied. "You'll just have to wait and see." She took a step back and crossed her arms against her body.

"I'm not good at waiting," Sam teased. "Especially when I want something and set my mind to get it."

Julie pretended not to understand his meaning. "You must have caused your family a great deal of trouble on Christmas morning."

"I was a perfect child," Sam grinned.

"I'm sure."

"Sure of what?" August asked as he came out the back door.

"Oh, never mind," Julie said with a sigh. "Would you mind helping Sam with the dogs while I get some of my gear?"

"You can just leave it all, and we'll bring it in," August said.

Sam laughed as Julie rolled her eyes. "Don't even start, August. She's got Christmas presents and doesn't want any of us to see them."

"Oh," August replied and went to unharness Kodiak.

Julie turned to Sam. "Now why can't you be more like him?" Sam shrugged his shoulders and went to help August.

Julie managed to get her gifts inside without running into her father. She was coming out of her room when Vern came in search of her.

"Jewels!" he said as he embraced her. "Good to have you home."

"Good to be home. I wanted to let you know about George Nakoota. He tangled with his dogs and had his arm ripped up pretty bad. I stitched him up, and it looks good for a full recovery."

"He was blessed to have you there," Vern said as he walked with Julie to the kitchen. "He probably would have died if you hadn't been. That village is nearly fifty miles from Nome, and he would have bled to death before he got proper care."

"Well, he's doing fine now, and I know he'll follow my instructions on how to care for the wounds. My biggest frustration with many of the Eskimos is their curiosity. I'll stitch something closed and bandage it up, and before I can recheck it, they've unbandaged it so they can see my handiwork."

Vern chuckled just as Sam and August came in through the back door. "You know where curiosity will get you," Vern added.

"Yeah," Sam answered with a grin. "No Christmas present."

Julie had brought extra sugar and eggs with her from Nome. She was determined to bake something nice for Christmas so she cleared the men from the kitchen.

Darkness fell by two o'clock, but Julie refused to let it dampen her spirits. It was Christmas Eve! She baked a cake and rolled out sugar cookies, a tradition started by her mother to pass the anxious hours.

As Julie used each of her mother's cookie cutters, she remembered with fondness the stories her mother would tell about them. The star was for the Bethlehem star that announced the birth of Christ. The Christmas tree, an outline of an evergreen, reminded them of everlasting life in Christ, and the shape of a bell was to bring to mind the joyous music in heaven whenever a sinner accepted Christ.

Taking a final batch of cookies from the oven, Julie put them aside to cool and turned her attention to the finishing touches on a chocolate cake. Setting out a stack of plates and forks, Julie went to the front room to retrieve the men.

"Who'd like some cake?" Julie asked as she entered the room.

"Cake? We should have Julie home more often," August said, deserting his chess game with Sam in order to take his sister's arm. "I'd love some, Julie. Lead the way."

"Yes," Sam said as he rushed to take Julie's other arm. "Lead the way."

Vern laughed and got to his feet. "I guess I'll just bring up the rear," he said and followed the trio into the kitchen.

They gathered around the table, praising the towering chocolate confectionery. Julie cut the cake and heaped huge slices of cake on each plate.

"Let's have the blessing," Vern suggested as Julie placed a pot of coffee on the table and went for cups.

Julie took a seat at the table. The men joined her and Vern led them in a short prayer.

"Father, we thank You for the birth of Your Son, Jesus, and the free gift of salvation which You gave to us through Him. Thank You for this gathering of loved ones as we celebrate that birth. Amen."

"What say we share our gifts now?" Vern suggested after a bite of cake. "Umm, Jewels, this is excellent."

"It sure is," August agreed. "And I agree with Pa. I'd like to exchange gifts."

Julie shrugged her shoulders. "I guess that's fine by me."

"Then I suggest everyone get their Christmas gifts, and we'll move to the front room," Vern said, adding, "Oh, and Julie, please bring the cake and coffee."

"I'll help her," Sam said as he got to his feet. "I'm trying to stay in Julie's good graces." He picked up the cake and coffee pot and moved to the front room.

Julie followed Sam with the coffee cups and then excused herself to retrieve her gifts. She unwrapped the fur bundle which she'd placed on her bed and revealed the guitar. The knife and tools were in separate boxes, so Julie rewrapped the guitar, tucked it under one arm, and grabbed the other gifts with her hands.

She joined the men in the living room and was surprised to find someone had decorated a small Christmas tree and placed it on a table in the center of the room. Beneath it were several wrapped packages of different sizes.

"How wonderful," Julie said as she placed her own gifts on the table. "I remember the last time we did this."

"It was the year before you left for Seattle," August said, taking a package from beneath the tree.

"Yes," Vern remembered, "and your mother was still here. I remember she made the most wonderful meal. I wish she could be here to enjoy this evening, but in a way, I guess she is."

"She sure is, Pa," Julie said as she took a seat on one of the overstuffed chairs opposite the couch.

"Here," August said handing his package to Julie. "I got this for you. Merry Christmas."

Julie opened the package to reveal a black lacquer jewelry box with beautiful red ornamentation. "Thank you, August. It's incredible." She opened the box to reveal a red velvet interior and added, "I've never seen anything like it."

"It's Japanese," August said proudly. "The guy I bought it from was trying to raise money to get home. He said it was one of a kind."

"Well, I haven't much in the way of jewelry, but I'll cherish it always," Julie said appreciatively. "That large bundle of fur over there is yours. But I need the wrapping back." She laughed.

August unwrapped the fur to reveal his gift. "A guitar! What a great idea, Jewels. Thanks," he said as he took the guitar out and began tightening the strings. "You didn't know I'd been taking lessons, did you?"

"Then you already have a guitar?" Julie asked disappointedly.

"No. I've been using Sam's."

"Sam's?" Julie said turning questioning eyes to Sam. "You truly are a man of surprises, Mr. Curtiss."

"You don't know the half of it, Miss Eriksson," Sam said with a laugh.

"Well, with both guitars here it would be a nice touch to our celebration if you'd both play us some Christmas songs," Vern proposed.

"Oh, yes, please!" Julie begged.

"Maybe after all the gifts are opened," Sam said and went to the table. "I have a gift for August as well."

He handed August a small package which when opened, revealed a dog harness. Vern and August exchanged curious glances, and Julie laughed as Sam, cleared up the mystery.

"Kodiak sired a litter of pups last fall, some of the best

quality dogs I've seen in a long time. I'm giving August his pick of the litter," Sam announced. "You've been a good friend, August." The men exchanged a heartfelt hug.

"A very generous gift indeed, friend," August stated, knowing Sam could sell any one of his dogs for better than a thousand dollars. "Thank you, Sam."

"You deserve it," Sam replied and took a seat by the fireplace.

"Well, I have a gift for my daughter," Vern said. He pulled several packages from beneath the tree and brought them to Julie.

"I feel like a little girl again," Julie said as she hurried to open each one. She immediately recognized the gifts as pieces of her mother's prized jewelry collection.

"Jewels for my jewel," Vern said and planted a kiss on Julie's forehead. "These were your mother's favorites."

"Yes, I know," Julie said with tears in her eyes. She held up a necklace against her white blouse. The gold of the chain and brilliance of the ruby settings looked good against Julie's dark hair.

"This was always my favorite one," Julie added as she replaced the ruby necklace, "because you gave it to her for Christmas not long after I turned sixteen. I thought it was the most romantic gift in all the world." She wiped at her eyes before looking into the other packages.

"Those pieces were some I thought you would enjoy. I thought I'd save the rest until you marry," Vern stated, wiping tears from his own eyes as well.

"Thank you, Papa," Julie said as she got up to retrieve her father's gift. "I'm afraid my present pales in comparison." She handed her father the package.

"I've already got the best gift in all the world. You've come home to Alaska, and that's enough for me."

As Julie watched her father unwrap the tools, she wondered if she should give Sam his gift. If she did and he hadn't gotten her anything for Christmas, he might feel bad. He might also take her gift the wrong way and think it was a promise of something more than friendship.

"Well, would you look at this," Vern said as he held up a new hammer. "I can't believe it, but they're exactly what I need. I was planning on buying all of these." Julie watched as he tested the blade of the saw and examined the chisel set. "Perfect!" Vern declared, and Julie leaned back feeling quite satisfied.

"Oh, I nearly forgot," Julie said as she got up and rushed to her room. She came back with the bundle which Tanana had given her. "These are from George's wife, Tanana. She thought I might not get a chance to do any Christmas shopping, and so she made these mukluks for me in pay for sewing up George."

"Anything that woman makes is a prize to be sure," Vern said as he undid the rawhide strip that tied the package shut. He examined the mukluks before passing one pair to August. "It also helps that she knows our sizes."

"Well, this has been a fine Christmas," Vern said as

he stretched out his feet.

"Wait," August said as he went to the tree. "There's another gift here. Who's this one for?"

Julie swallowed hard. It was now or never, she decided and quickly answered. "That one is for Sam."

Three pairs of eyes turned in surprise at her, and Julie wished she could crawl beneath the chair. "I never had a chance to properly thank him for all he did for me. Merry Christmas, Sam," she said quickly to break the tension.

"Well, I must say this is a surprise," Sam said as he accepted the package from August. He unwrapped the brown paper to reveal the knife and sheath. "It's exquisite," he murmured as he examined the craftsmanship. "I've never had one as fine. Thank you, Julie."

She blushed under the intensity of Sam's eyes. The silence was unbearable, and Julie searched her mind for something to say. "How about those songs, now?" she finally questioned.

"Yes," Vern agreed, "now would be the perfect time." He leaned his head back and closed his eyes.

"I'll get your guitar, Sam," August offered and went to his room.

Sam studied the knife before sheathing it and looping it onto his belt. He was more than touched at Julie's extravagant gift. It signaled a change in their relationship. Had Julie come to approve of the idea of marriage? He couldn't wait until a time revealed itself when he could be alone and offer his own Christmas gift.

After several hours of listening to Sam and August, as well as joining in on all the songs they could think to sing, Vern suggested they read the nativity story. Everyone readily agreed, and while Sam continued to strum the haunting melody of "Silent Night," Vern, August, and Julie took turns reading the second chapter of Luke.

When they'd finished, Vern offered a prayer and got up to stretch. "I think I'm going to retire, but before I do, I'd like to say something. I wasn't looking forward to this holiday. It was always Agneta's favorite, and I knew that it wouldn't be the same without her. But I was wrong. The celebration of Christ's birth isn't a matter of the house you live in or the people who share your table. It's a matter of the heart. If the Lord lives here," Vern said as he patted his chest with his hand, "then Christmas is a matter of everyday life. Agneta would want it that way, too. Good night."

Julie watched her father walk from the room. She admired his strength and, in it, found more courage for herself.

"Unless you need help cleaning up, I'm going to bed, too," August said as he ran a gentle hand over the guitar. "This is a swell gift, Jewels. I'm going to enjoy it for a long, long time."

"I'm glad you like it," Julie said, getting up to embrace her brother. "You go ahead to bed. I can manage all of this just fine. Besides, I want to see if the aurora makes an appearance tonight." August nodded, gave Sam a single-fingered salute, and took his leave.

Julie knew that Sam's eyes were on her even before she turned around. What would she say to him? How could she deal with the feelings her heart would no longer let her deny? She cared for Sam, that much was true. But how would it fit in with her nursing? Was it really love she felt or merely infatuation? Taking a deep breath, she turned to meet his eyes.

"Do you have to clear these things away just yet?" Sam asked as he came across the room.

"No," Julie whispered. "I suppose they can wait."

"Good, because I can't," Sam said and took Julie in his arms. His kiss was as gentle as the first he'd ever given her, but the feelings he evoked in Julie's heart were so much greater.

After what seemed an eternity, Julie pushed away. "I can't breathe," she laughed, trying hard to push aside the passion she was feeling.

Sam allowed her the space and led her to the couch. "I want to talk to you," he said as he sat down beside her. "I have a Christmas gift for you."

"You shouldn't have," Julie said in a barely audible voice. Having Sam so close completely muddled her thoughts.

Sam reached into his pocket and pulled out a small box. He opened it for Julie and revealed a ring of gold, with a small diamond. "Julie," he whispered, "will you marry me?"

Julie stared dumfoundedly at the box. He'd actually proposed. None of his presumptuous attitudes or the self-assured cockiness that he'd delivered before, just the plain and simple heart of the matter. A marriage proposal!

"I don't know what to say."

"Say, yes," Sam said as he took the ring from the box and slipped it on Julie's finger.

Julie stared at the ring for several minutes. It was a bit big, but it was exactly what Julie would have hoped for in a wedding ring.

"We've only known each other a couple of months," Julie said, searching for a way she could avoid dealing with the issue.

"We both know it's right," Sam said as he pulled Julie against him. "I love you, Julie, and whether or not you'll admit it, I know you love me."

Julie trembled in Sam's arms. Her breath caught in her throat and made it impossible to deny his statement. Did she love him?

"I don't know what I'm feeling," Julie finally answered honestly. "I won't deny the chemistry between us, but Sam, you weren't in my plans."

"What about God's plans?"

"But I thought I knew what God's plans for me were," Julie said, daring to look into Sam's piercing brown eyes. "I thought I knew exactly what I was supposed to do."

"And now?" Sam questioned.

"Now," Julie said as she took off the ring. "I feel confused. I can't marry you, Sam, unless I know for sure it's what I'm supposed to do." She handed him the ring, expecting an angry retort. Instead, Sam surprised her.

Closing his hand around Julie's fingers and the ring, he spoke. "Keep the ring. I feel confident that God has sent you to be my wife. One day, you'll know it too, and you'll come to me wearing it, and I'll know your answer." With that, Sam placed a light kiss on Julie's forehead and got up. "Goodnight, love," he said and left Julie to contemplate her feelings.

Julie held the ring tightly and prayed. "Oh, God, what am I to do? I thought the way was so clear. You had shone a light of understanding on the path that I was to take, and I felt confident that I was making the right choice. Now," she paused and looked at the ring. "Now, I just don't know. I'm so afraid, and I need to understand what I'm to do. I want to serve you, Father. I want to bring glory to you. Can I do this as Sam's wife?"

Several minutes passed. With the ring still in her hand, Julie retrieved her father's Bible and opened it to Joshua 1:9: "Have I not commanded thee? Be strong and of a good courage; be not afraid, neither be thou dismayed: for the Lord thy God is with thee whithersoever thou goest."

"I won't be afraid," Julie said as she reread the verse. "You have commanded me to be strong and with Your help, Father, I will be." Peace filled Julie's heart. "I don't know what the answer is regarding Sam, Lord. But You do, and I am Your servant, seeking to know Your will. Open my heart to Your direction, so that my own plans won't thwart the divine ones You have ordained for me. Amen."

ten

January 1925 started out cold, with the mercury dipping to thirty below zero. Julie took extra precautions to maintain warmth and safety on the trail by carrying more blankets, additional food, and dry fuel for fires.

She had read several articles in the *Nome Nugget* of the Army's findings while experimenting with temperature in the far north. Apparently, it wasn't enough to calculate the outside temperature when determining how dangerous conditions were. The speed of the wind had to be considered as well. The Army had concluded that while a fifteen degree temperature seemed warm to the natives of Nome, if the wind were blowing at ten to twelve miles an hour, it would feel more like forty below zero. Something call wind chill, Julie remembered, and it could create problems for a person on the trail.

The snow had been sporadic that winter, and Nome's streets weren't buried as deeply as they usually were at the first of the year. Julie knew that however good conditions were in Nome, she had no way to tell what would greet her as she mushed out across the less-traveled trails.

"We haven't had any traffic from the west or north," she said as she finished her coffee one morning with Dr.

Welch and his wife. "So I have no way of knowing what the trails are like."

"I wish I could go with you," Dr. Welch replied honestly. He loved to mush his dogs and found city life a bit stifling at times.

"Actually, I wish you could, too," Julie said with a smile for Dr. Welch's wife. "I love to watch your husband at work, Mrs. Welch."

"Now, Julie, I think we've been friends far too long to continue with the 'Mrs. Welch' title. Just call me Lula; all my friends do."

"I like to call her Lu," Dr. Welch said with a fond smile for his wife, "among other things."

"You're being quite impossible today, Dr. Welch," Lula said with a teasing note to her voice. "You're probably better off with him staying in Nome, Julie. I have a feeling he'd want to wander off and do some ice fishing or visit, if he went on the trail."

Julie laughed and glanced at her watch. It wouldn't be light for another three hours, but the trail beckoned. "I'm going to have to be on my way. Thanks again for the coffee, Lula," she said, trying the name for the first time. "I should be back in a few weeks."

Just then a loud knock at the door caught their attention. "A doctor's house is an open arena," Lula said with a smile. "I'll just see who that might be."

Lula Welch opened the door to reveal an Eskimo man. "I have sick children," he said in a worried way that caused Dr. Welch to jump to his feet.

"What seems to be wrong?" he questioned the man, as Lula brought his fur parka.

"They're burning with fever, and their throats are sore," the man answered.

"How old are they?" Dr. Welch questioned. Lula brought his medical bag and set it on the table.

"One's three, and my baby is only one year old. Can you help them, Doctor? I don't have much money, but I can work hard for you."

Dr. Welch waved the man's concerns away. "Nonsense. We'll discuss such matters later. First, let's see if we can figure out how to help the little ones." He planted a kiss on Lula's temple and turned to Julie. "You can always send me a radio message through the Army Signal Corps, should you need anything or have a problem."

"I'll keep that in mind," Julie said. She pulled on her parka and secured the hood. "Would you like me to drive you to the settlement?"

"No," Dr. Welch said shaking his head. "There's not so much snow as to impede a good walk, and I need the exercise. Thanks anyway." With that, Dr. Welch hastened into the darkness with the fearful father.

"I guess I'd better be on my way as well," Julie remarked. "I'll be in touch. Thanks again for the coffee."

"We'll look forward to seeing you when you get back," Lula said as she followed Julie to the door. "Be careful."

"I will be," Julie promised and took herself out into the darkness.

The town was quiet, even though there was plenty of activity. Julie felt an emptiness as she watched couples making their way into nearby shops. Maybe she wasn't cut out for public health nursing after all. While she loved nursing and working with the Eskimos, the long, lonely hours on the trail were difficult.

Images of Sam filled Julie's mind. She thought of the ring that lay securely at the bottom of her knapsack. It was a symbol of Sam's devotion. Would she ever be able to put the ring on and give Sam the answer he longed to hear?

In the back of her mind, Julie remembered the verses from Ecclesiastes that her father had read. "Two are better than one. . . . For if they fall, the one will lift up his fellow: but woe to him that is alone when he falleth; for he hath not another to help him up." Loneliness penetrated her heart.

Julie consoled herself with the idea of stopping at home before pushing west. Maybe she could talk to her father about Sam's proposal and her loneliness. He could offer her some idea of what she should do.

Julie checked the tarp covering her supplies and, when she was certain that everything was secure, she took to the back of her sled.

"Were you planning on leaving without saying good-bye?" Sam questioned as he placed his hands on Julie's shoulders.

Julie turned. Dim light illuminated Sam's bearded face. His hair had been neatly cut and his beard trimmed. He was quite handsome, Julie decided. She could do much worse.

"I can't always be looking over my shoulder for you, every time I'm about to go on my route," Julie said, trying to distance herself from the emotions Sam stirred within her.

"I thought you were avoiding me," Sam countered. "I don't suppose you've given much thought to my proposal."

"I've, uh, well," Julie stammered, "I've been busy with my nursing. Since the first part of the month, I've been working with Dr. Welch and haven't even managed to get home. I also have several villages to the northwest to attend to, so you can see I've been very busy."

"That doesn't answer my question," Sam remarked.

"I think it should," Julie said nervously. "I've been too busy to see my family. Doesn't it seem reasonable that I've been too busy to consider your marriage proposal?"

"No," Sam said firmly. "It doesn't."

Julie's mouth opened in surprise. She had banked on Sam's good nature making him drop the issue. Instead he remained a determined force to be reckoned with.

"Do you have any idea what my nursing means to me?" Julie asked seriously. *Perhaps,* she thought, *if Sam knew what my responsibilities mean to me, he'd understand my hesitation.*

"Do you have any idea what you mean to me?" Sam said as he moved closer. His warm breath formed frosty white steam in the morning cold.

"That's not fair, Sam. I asked you first."

"If I answer you, will you give me an answer?" Sam questioned. "I think it's only fair."

"I imagine I mean something quite special to you. After all, you did ask me to marry you," Julie stated evenly. "Now, I've answered your question. Will you answer mine?"

Sam chuckled. "Your father was right. You are something else when you have a full head of steam. Sometime, you'll have to tell me what happened when your father wanted to shoot that pup. No doubt you didn't cut him any more maneuvering room than you are me."

Julie smiled ruefully. "My father told me that pup was good for nothing but taking up space and eating. He said he couldn't be expected to pull his own weight, much less that of a sled. I told him I wasn't all that different. I was too young to bring in any wealth to the family, and certainly I wasn't capable of pulling my own weight. I put myself between the pup and my father's leveled gun and told him he might as well do away with both of us, because the weak were worthless when it came to surviving in the north."

Sam smiled at her determination. "I guess I don't have to ask what happened."

"My father relented. Told me I was spoiled and," Julie added with amusement, "he made me take care of the pup."

"How'd it work out?"

"My father knew best," Julie said sadly. "The pup got in a fight with some of the other dogs. They killed him."

"I'm sorry," Sam replied honestly.

"I learned a good lesson," Julie said as she shook the image from her mind. "Never once did my father tell me, 'I told you so.' He put his arm around me and let me cry. Then he shared the words of Proverbs 1:8: 'My son, hear the instruction of thy father, and forsake not the law of thy mother.' He told me it counted for daughters as well."

"Your father is a wise man," Sam said softly.

"Yes, he is," Julie agreed, "and that's exactly why I need to talk to him before I can give you any kind of an answer."

"I see," Sam answered thoughtfully. "I suppose it wouldn't help if I told you that I've already talked to him about it."

"What?" Julie's head snapped up.

"I talked to your father before I ever asked you to marry me," Sam replied. "I wouldn't have dreamed of approaching you with a proposal unless I was certain your father approved."

"And did he?"

Sam smiled and reached out a hand to push back Julie's hood. "He told me it was up to you."

"That's it?" Julie questioned as she took a step back to avoid Sam's touch. "He didn't say anything else?"

"Should he have?"

"I don't know. I guess I just wondered if he—"

"If he had an answer for you?" Sam interrupted. "I didn't ask your father to marry me. I only sought his blessing. It's you I want an answer from."

Julie turned away from Sam and rechecked her sled harness. Part of her wanted to tell Sam no, but no matter how she tried, Julie couldn't form the word. Why couldn't she simply refuse to marry him and let him slip from her life? "I don't have an answer for you, Sam," she finally said.

"Do you know when you might?"

Julie straightened up slowly, avoiding his eyes.

"Look at me, Julie," Sam said as he reached out and turned her to face him. "This should be a happy experience for both of us. It should be a wonderful and joyful event for two people who love each other. You do love me, don't you?" It was more a statement than a question.

Julie took a deep breath to steady herself. That was the important question. Did she love Sam?

"I—"

"Say, aren't you Julie Eriksson?" a voice called out from behind Sam. Julie recognized the bulky form of her father's long time friend, Jonah Emery.

"Hello, Jonah," Julie said sweetly, grateful for the reprieve.

"I heard you were back in these parts as a nurse. Say,

I'll bet your Papa is mighty proud."

"I'll say he is," Sam joined in.

"Why, Sam Curtiss, I should have known that towering frame belonged to you. Well, I'll let you two get back to your discussion," Jonah said with a wave. "You be sure and tell your pa hello from me."

"I will," Julie promised and watched as Jonah moved down the street to one of the small cafes.

"I'm still waiting for my answer," Sam said as Julie turned back to face him.

"I can't give you an answer."

"Then when, Julie?"

She thought for a moment. "I'm going to be gone for a month, maybe more. I'll have an answer for you when I return."

Sam grinned and pulled Julie into his arms. "Then let me give you a reminder to take on the trail," he whispered and lowered his lips to kiss her.

Julie stepped back breathlessly, even though the kiss was brief. She looked apprehensively up and down the street to see if anyone had seen Sam kiss her. When she turned back to reprimand Sam for his behavior, he was gone.

Balancing between relief and disappointment, Julie quickly wrapped several scarves around her face and secured her hood. She could only pray that God would provide her an answer to Sam's question.

"Mush!" she called out and held on tightly as the dogs fairly burst from the start.

From the dark haven of the entryway to a store, Sam watched Julie move down the street and out of sight. It was hard to let her go without demanding that she accept his love and affection, but Sam had made God a promise. "Thy will be done," Sam whispered in the darkness. "Thy will be done."

eleven

Troubled by her promise to Sam, Julie forgot about going home. She mushed out of Nome on trails that took her west along the ice-packed Bering Sea. The coastline trails were easy to follow, and they often moved off the banks onto the frozen sea itself. This helped drivers avoid heavily drifted snow and hidden obstacles.

Out on the ice, Julie had new concerns to keep her mind on. The wind and pressure often caused the ice to form what the natives called "spears." These ice needles jutted upward from the frozen trail and could pierce the padding of a dog's feet. Whenever spears were evident, Julie took time out to put coverings on the paws of each of her dogs. So far, they'd avoided injury.

As the dimly lit skies gave way to sunlight, Julie pushed back her parka hood. She could tell by the dogs' breath that the temperature had risen. A good driver always paid attention to the degree of whiteness that showed in a team's exhaled breath. Little things like that often saved a driver's life, and Julie, ever mindful of her near death from the blizzard, paid special attention to such details.

The ice and snow stretched for miles, and the glare of reflecting sunlight caused Julie to shelter her eyes by replacing her hood.

The team moved at a nice trot, and Julie felt exhilarated as she made her way down the coastline. The hills and mountains in the distance, however, reminded her of the dangers that came with isolation. One mistake could be her last.

Thinking about mistakes, Julie considered Sam's marriage proposal. "Lord," she prayed, "I don't know what to do about Sam. He says he loves me, but I don't know if I love him. I suppose I shouldn't be so worried about it—after all, Sam is a Christian."

The miles passed in a blur as Julie continued, "I don't know what to do! My job as a public health nurse takes me out on the trail for weeks, even months at a time. How can I be a good wife to a man while I'm hundreds of miles away inoculating children and teaching mothers about hygiene? Sam deserves more than a pittance of attention every few weeks. I'm sure a man with his zest for living would expect a great deal more, Father. I know he would, and I'd feel obligated to give it to him and leave my job. Since I can't do that, it must be wrong for me to accept his proposal."

That conclusion didn't last long. Unsettled feelings in Julie's mind told her that the issue was far from being resolved.

Sam's never suggested I leave my work as a nurse, she reasoned. *Even when he bids me good-bye, he never causes a scene about my work or says that I ought to be safe at home. Maybe Sam is more sympathetic to the needs of the people up here. Maybe Sam would want me to continue working as a public health nurse, even after we were married.*

"So the answer must be yes," Julie said aloud, but again the feeling that the issue wasn't settled came to haunt her.

"Do I love him?" she asked.

She thought of the way he smiled and the laughter in his brown eyes. The vision of Sam's muscular shoulders and towering frame came to mind. Julie admitted to herself that she was attracted to Sam as she'd never been to another man. *Attraction isn't love*, she reminded herself. *But is it part of love?*

Julie's mittened hands twisted at the sled bar. She couldn't settle on any answers to her many questions.

"Please, Lord, I promised him an answer. Please show me whether or not I love him. I must know that before I can answer his proposal because I simply cannot marry a man I do not love."

The daylight hours passed much too quickly. In the distance, Julie saw the flickering light of a lantern hanging on a pole outside a sod igloo. She sighed in relief, eager to rest after only two short stops on the trail.

The village wouldn't recognize their new public health nurse, but Julie knew she'd be warmly welcomed. She halted the dogs as several Eskimos appeared.

"I'm Nurse Eriksson from Nome," Julie offered by way of introduction.

"We're glad to have you," an older man said as he

extended his hand. "We have sickness in our village. It is good you have come."

"If you will lend me a warm place to work," Julie said as she reached for her gear, "I'll be glad to examine your sick."

The man nodded and pointed to the sod igloo. "You use my house. I have no wife. I will stay with my brother and his family while you work. Come."

"Thank you," Julie said as she followed the man. "What should I call you?"

The man turned and smiled, revealing several missing teeth. "Call me Charlie," he said and showed Julie inside the shack.

Julie was appalled by what greeted her. The igloo was filthy and very small, leaving her to wonder if these conditions were common in the rest of the village. She noticed the small oil can stove and turned to Charlie.

"Is there fuel for the stove?"

"Sure," Charlie replied. "I get you nice fire. Plenty warm in here with big fire."

"I'll need water, too," Julie said as she pulled her parka off. It was chilly, but not unbearable, and once she began to clean the room, her body would warm considerably.

"I get you plenty snow, and we melt on big fire. You can have much hot water."

Charlie seemed so pleased to offer Julie his home that she didn't want to hurt his feelings by rearranging everything. "Would it be all right," she began, "if I clean this table so that I can examine the patients?"

"Sure, sure," Charlie said with his broad toothless smile. "You have plenty fire, plenty water, and plenty clean. Sure."

Charlie disappeared out the door, and Julie could hear him talking excitedly to the villagers. He reappeared and within minutes had a nice fire going in the stove as well as several pans of snow melting on top of it.

Julie rolled up the sleeves of her heavy flannel shirt. While nurses in Nome's hospital wore a recognizable uniform, Julie wore what best suited the climate and elements she would have to combat; warm flannels and wools along with furs and skin pants were of much more benefit to her near the Bering Sea than starched aprons and freshly pressed dresses. She was just pinning up her hair when a young woman burst through the door with her infant child in hand.

"My baby is sick," she cried as she held the infant up to Julie.

Julie reached for the child. His burning skin told her that he had a dangerously high fever.

"How long has he been sick?" Julie questioned the mother while examining the baby.

"He's had a bad cold for two days. He breathes so hard I can't rest for fear he'll stop breathing," the little Eskimo woman said as she twisted her hands.

Julie could hear the labored, shallow breathing of the infant. He was perilously close to death. But why? Julie couldn't find any obvious reason for the baby to be so ill. "I must look in his mouth," Julie told his mother as she pulled a tongue depressor from her bag. "I won't hurt him, but he won't like it." Julie doubted that the lethargic baby would fight her, but she felt better warning the mother about her actions.

The light was so poor that Julie could scarcely see past the child's tongue and gums. "I need more light," she called to Charlie and waited until he brought her a lantern.

"Plenty light for the nurse," Charlie said and went back to his self-assigned task of melting snow at the stove.

Julie positioned the light to give her a good view into the child's mouth. She pried the tiny mouth open and gasped. The back of the child's swollen throat was covered with gray-white patches of dead mucous membrane, the unmistakable calling card of diphtheria. Julie looked up sympathetically at the frantically worried young mother. How could she explain to the woman that her baby would probably die that night?

"Are there any others in the village with this sickness?" Julie asked.

"Yes, there are two other children with sore throats and high fevers," the woman answered. "Can you make my baby well?"

Julie felt the pain displayed in the woman's eyes. "No, I'm sorry. Your baby is very sick, and I can't help him. We've waited too long, and I don't have the medicine I need to help you."

The woman's anxious face fell into complete dejection. She grabbed up her baby and began to wail. Charlie came from the stove and asked Julie what was wrong with the baby.

"It's a white man's disease called diphtheria," Julie said as the crying mother rocked back and forth, cradling her dying child. "I need medicine from Nome in order to save the people from getting the disease. The ones who are already sick may not have enough time left for me to get back and help them. Charlie, I'm going to need your help. Do you have a village council?"

"Sure, sure," Charlie said repeating what appeared to be his favorite word. "We got plenty people on council."

"I need you to call them together. This disease is very contagious. That means it spreads quickly. Charlie, we mustn't let anyone come into the village or leave it. Do you understand? I have to go back to Nome and get the antitoxin."

"Sure, Charlie understand plenty good," the old man said with a grave nod. "I keep people here, and nobody else come in."

"Good," Julie replied. "Charlie, I need to have the dogs ready to leave in ten minutes. Can you have them for me?"

"Sure, but you plenty tired. You need rest to travel," Charlie answered in a way that reminded Julie of her father.

"Yes, Charlie, I know. But if I don't get the medicine

and get right back to the village, many of your people will die. I have to try."

"You try then," Charlie said and patted Julie on the back. "But you don't take the ice. Big wind blowing off the water is making it soft. It might be gone in the night."

"Thank you, Charlie. I'll stick to the land trail," Julie promised.

After speaking with the council about quarantining the homes of the sick and leaving instructions on how to ease the sufferings of those with the disease, Julie repacked her supplies and readied her sled.

Starting with Dusty, Julie lovingly patted her dogs and checked them for any signs of stiffness or injury. Eager to be back on the trail, the dogs seemed to understand the importance of their mission.

Julie moved her team out and ran alongside the sled for quite a distance. She wanted to insure that she stayed warm, so she only rode the runners when fatigue threatened her with exhaustion. In record time, she saw the lights of Nome and breathed a prayer of thanksgiving.

Julie pushed the dogs to Dr. Welch's house. Mindless of the hour, she pounded on the door. Surprisingly, Dr. Welch himself appeared at the door, fully dressed.

"Julie, come inside. What is it?" Dr. Welch questioned as he ushered the girl to a seat by the stove.

"Diphtheria! The Sinuak village has several cases. One will certainly not make it through the night, and the others I doubt I can help either. I came back for antitoxin."

Dr. Welch looked old beyond his years. Julie worried for his health as he ran a hand through his graying hair and sat down at the kitchen table. "I haven't got any. At least not enough."

"How much do you have?" Julie questioned in a worried tone that matched the doctor's.

"We only have 75,000 units, and I already have cases of diphtheria appearing here in Nome. The two children I was called to care for are dead. I didn't know then that it was diphtheria, as I couldn't get a look inside their mouths. However, little Richard Stanley is also sick, and I saw quite well the patches on his throat. It's diphtheria, all right."

"What are we to do?" Julie asked as she joined the doctor at the table.

"I don't know," the doctor answered bluntly. "It takes 30,000 units of antitoxin to treat one sick person. I've already got at least four who are sick with the disease and hundreds of others who are exposed."

"To make matters worse," Lula Welch said as she appeared in her nightgown and robe, "the serum we have on hand is over five years old. We'd hoped that the Public Health Department had sent some with you when you returned from Seattle, but they must have been short on it themselves. We didn't receive a single unit."

Julie sat back and took a deep breath. "So we don't know if the serum on hand is effective?"

"That's about the whole of it," Dr. Welch said and put his head in his hands. "We must be prepared to deal with a full-scale epidemic. Diphtheria will only take a matter of days to spread like a flame on dried kindling. The entire peninsula is in danger of epidemic. God help us."

"Yes, He's our only hope now," Julie agreed. "He's our only hope!"

twelve

Julie stayed at the Welch home, and that morning word came that little Richard Stanley had passed away in the night. There was nothing left to do, Dr. Welch decided, but to call upon the mayor and announce an epidemic.

Sitting in the office of the *Nome Nugget*, all eyes of the city council turned to the publisher, George Maynard. As well as operating and publishing Nome's only newspaper, George Maynard was also the town's mayor.

"Diphtheria? Are you sure, Curt?" George questioned Dr. Welch. "We haven't had diphtheria in these parts for over twenty years, and with the ports all frozen up, how would we get the serum now?"

"I can't tell you the hows and whys, but facts are facts. I wish it weren't so, but the truth of the matter is I've already got three dead children to prove my diagnosis. I'm getting more reports of people taken with fever and sore throat. Frankly, George, it's going to get a whole lot worse before it gets better."

"But don't we have an injection for that kind of thing?" the mayor asked with a hopeful expression.

"We do, and we don't," Dr. Welch explained as he rubbed his eyes with the backs of his hands. "There is an antitoxin, but Nome doesn't have it."

"What are you saying?" M. L. Summers, superintendent of the Hammon Consolidated Gold Fields, questioned.

"I'm saying we have an epidemic, and people are dying. Further more, there is a cure, but we don't have it within reach. I have a small amount of antitoxin, but it's over five years old and probably ineffective. There's certainly not enough to stave off an epidemic."

"What do you suggest we do, Doc?" Sam asked as he moved forward from the back of the room.

"We have to quarantine the sick and keep people from spreading the disease. The first order of business is to close the schools and the movie theater," Dr. Welch said as he leaned back in his chair. "As this region's director of public health, I would also like to have a board of health formed to enforce the quarantine. We can't have anybody coming in or going out of Nome."

"Summers, you could take that job on, couldn't you?" Mayor Maynard asked.

"Certainly," Summers answered, feeling honored to be put in the position.

"I'll run a quarantine notice on the front page," Maynard said as he jotted down notes on a pad of paper.

"Thank you," Dr. Welch replied.

"What else can we do?" Sam questioned.

"The biggest problem we have on hand is how to get the antitoxin. I haven't any idea where there might be a supply large enough to help us. It might be in Fairbanks or Anchorage. Then again it might be as far away as Juneau or Seattle. Regardless, when we locate the serum we'll have another problem on our hands: how do we get it here?"

"If we can locate serum in either Anchorage or Fairbanks," Mayor Maynard began, "there might be a pilot daring enough to fly it to us." Everyone looked skeptical at the suggestion. Flying was new enough to the States, but in Alaska, it was almost unheard of, especially in the winter.

"That might work if it were summer, but I don't think we can afford to risk it in the middle of winter. There's no way of knowing if those engines can handle thirty or forty below zero," one of the other council members said. Murmurs filled the room as the men concurred that flight might be a bad notion.

"Look," Sam said, suddenly getting an idea, "what if we used dog teams? We know they can make it through on the mail routes from Fairbanks. If Fairbanks has the serum, we could start it mushing west and send someone out to meet it. Maybe even relay it across the territory."

"But that will take nearly a month," the mayor argued.

"Not if we send Leonhard Seppala," Summers said, getting to his feet. "You all know he's the best musher in Alaska. His Siberian huskies are faster than any other team around these parts." The council members nodded as Summers continued. "Seppala works for me, and I would gladly allow him the time to perform this courageous act."

"Yeah, those little plume-tailed rats might just pull it

off. So we start someone out from Fairbanks with the serum and—"

"So far there is no serum," Sam interrupted the mayor. "We have to send out a radio message and find the serum before we can move it to Nome."

"Sam's right," Dr. Welch said with a nod of his head. "We have to locate the serum first, and then worry about how to get it here."

"Whatever it takes," Maynard said as he pounded his fist on the table. "No matter the cost. We all remember the influenza epidemic of 1919."

"Yes, and it didn't help much that the outside had already had its death tolls from it the year before," Welch added. "We were no better prepared for that epidemic than we are for this one."

"Dr. Welch, you give a message to the U.S. Army Signal Corps radiotelegraph station. We're behind you one hundred percent. Just let us know what we need to do," the mayor replied.

"I'll take you there, Doc. My team's right outside the door," Sam said as he got up to retrieve his parka.

"Very well, gentlemen. I will rely upon you to work with our new board of health director and the mayor as we strive to take control of this nightmare." Dr. Welch got to his feet and followed Sam to where the coats had been haphazardly thrown to one side.

"I'll keep all of you informed," Welch promised and followed Sam out the door.

"This must go priority to Juneau, Fairbanks, Anchorage, and Seward," Dr. Welch instructed as he handed a piece of paper to the sergeant who manned the radiotelegraph station.

Sergeant James Anderson took the paper and read it, paling slightly as he finished its contents. "Looks like we're in for it, huh, Doc?"

"That it does," Dr. Welch said as he cast a side glance at Sam.

Sam was deep in thought over concern for the town of Nome, but especially for Julie. He wished it were possible to make the serum appear on the next mail delivery, but wishing wouldn't make it so.

"I'll notify my superiors, and we'll have a man stationed here twenty-four-hours-a-day until we receive an answer," the sergeant said as he prepared to telegraph the message.

Sam watched the man put on his headset. Turning the dial to turn the frequency, the man began the message. "-./—/—/. -.-./.-/.-../.-../.-./—." The radio key clicked out the words, "Nome, calling."

The room seemed shrouded in silence against the rhythmic tapping of the telegraph key. Sam and Dr. Welch stood to one side as the sergeant tapped out the call again. He paused and waited to see if anyone would pick up his signal.

Within seconds the answer tapped back. "Fairbanks, calling. Go ahead, Nome."

The sergeant turned and nodded to Dr. Welch. "It's Fairbanks. I'll relay the message."

The sergeant's finger tapped out the message with expert ease. "Nome, calling. We have an outbreak of diphtheria. No serum. Urgently need help."

Sam and Dr. Welch breathed a sigh of relief. Just knowing that the rest of the word would learn of their need gave them hope.

The sergeant continued to radio the message to Anchorage, Juneau, and Seward. "I'll let you know when I get anything in," Sergeant Anderson said as he took off his head set.

"Thanks, Sergeant," Sam said and offered his dog team to Dr. Welch.

For days, time stood still in Nome. The only thing that didn't slow was the diphtheria. Three children were dead, ten new active cases were revealed, and more than fifty people reported they'd been exposed. Dr. Welch could only use what little serum he had on hand. Soon not a single unit remained.

Finally, on January 25, a message was received in Nome. Anchorage had 300,000 units of serum at the Alaska Railroad Hospital. It could be packaged and loaded on the number sixty-six Anchorage-to-Fairbanks Passenger Special and received at the Nenana railhead within two days. The Star Route of the interior mail delivery mushed out by dog sled from Nenana and could carry the serum with it as part of its load.

Dr. Welch gave the go ahead, and Sergeant Anderson wired the message to Dr. Beeson in Anchorage to proceed with the shipment.

"I suggest we call a city council meeting," Dr. Welch said as the sergeant finished his message. "This presents a whole new problem."

Within an hour, everyone had gathered for the meeting. Julie stood to one side of the meeting hall, while Sam kept determined eyes on her from the opposite side of the room. It was the first time he'd seen her since she'd left for her routes. She'd done nothing to let him know of her hurried return to Nome.

It was also the first time Sam had seen Julie in a dress. Self-consciously, Julie smoothed the white uniform, mindful of the way it displayed her more feminine qualities. She was wearing her uniform because she'd been helping at the hospital with the non-diphtheria patients. Dr. Welch had wisely kept the hospital quarantined for those patients whose ills did not involve diphtheria and required surgery or detailed medical help. Nurse Seville had been dispatched to the Sinuak village to work with the natives while Julie stayed on in Nome.

"I know you've all been waiting for good news," Dr. Welch began, "and finally I have some to report. Anchorage has 300,000 units of serum, and they've started it north to Nenana on the train." A cry of excited voices went up. Dr. Welch waited until the crowd had quieted before continuing. "We must decide how we are to get the serum from Nenana to Nome. Anchorage advises me that it will arrive in Nenana tomorrow."

"Leonhard Seppala has agreed to go after the serum,"

M. L. Summers announced.

"The arrangements have already been made to start the serum west after Nenana," Dr. Welch declared. "Several relay teams will work it down the Tanana and Yukon Rivers. Perhaps we could have Seppala meet the serum, say at Nulato?"

"That's over six hundred miles round trip," Sam advised. "It would be a hardship for one man and one team of dogs."

"Seppala suggests he take a team of thirty or so dogs," Summers expounded. "He would drop dogs off at the various roadhouses and cabins along the route and pick them up fresh on the way back. That way he could mush night and day. He believes it would only take a return trip of three, maybe four days."

"Three or four days?" one of the other men questioned. "That would average nearly one hundred miles a day! Seppala's huskies are good, but they're not indestructible."

"Have him stand by," Dr. Welch said as he contemplated the matter. "I'm still awaiting word from the governor. I'm not authorized to make the decision on my own."

The men nodded and settled down. Julie took the opportunity to slip quietly from the room in order to avoid Sam, but he was prepared for her action and followed her out. Julie was halfway down the hall and heading for her parka when Sam caught hold of her arm and whirled her into his arms.

"You look incredible," he whispered against her ear.

Julie thrilled to his touch, melting at once against his lean, muscular form. How often had she dreamed of this during those lonely nights spent out on the trail.

"You know," Sam said with a teasing smile, "I never purchase a sled dog sight unseen. I always go over them with a well-trained eye, just in case there are any hidden defects. But you, I was ready to take sight unseen, buried under pounds of furs and leather. Boy, was that a good call!"

"I beg your pardon," Julie said indignantly and pushed away. "Are you comparing your marriage proposal to purchasing a dog?" She clamped her hand automatically over her mouth, grimacing because the very subject she'd hoped to avoid was now open for conversation.

"You know I didn't mean it that way. I just can't believe how beautiful you look in that dress. Now come here, and give me a kiss."

Julie shook her head and backed away. "Remember the quarantine," she said firmly.

"I do," Sam said as he moved forward.

"No close physical contact," Julie reminded.

"Uh huh," Sam agreed, all the while moving forward at a steady pace.

"You aren't going to break the rules," Julie asked as she came to a stop against the wall, "are you?"

"Yup," Sam said and pulled her against him tightly. "If love could kill a man, I'd already be dead," he said as he lowered his mouth to Julie's and kissed her soundly.

Julie's mind went blank as her senses came alive. What was the cologne Sam was wearing, and why hadn't she noticed before how soft his beard was?

Voices down the hall brought Julie back to her senses. She pushed at Sam with both hands and gasped for air. "I've got to get back to work," she said and maneuvered under his sinewy arms.

"We can, uh, talk later," she said, pulling on her parka and acknowledging Dr. Welch as he approached.

Sam grinned at her embarrassment, but let it go at that. He'd have plenty of time later.

thirteen

By the morning of January 30, Leonhard Seppala had been given the go-ahead and had moved his huskies out across the trail to press ever closer to the serum.

The people of Nome were frantic. There had been five deaths, twenty-two active cases, and thirty-some suspected cases of diphtheria. All they could do was wait and make those who were ill as comfortable as possible.

Julie was working with Dr. Welch when Sergeant Anderson arrived with a message from Territorial Governor Scott Bone. He was requesting that more relays be set up between Nulato and Nome, as the Army reported a severe change in the weather.

"This isn't good," Dr. Welch said as he motioned Julie to follow him. "Sergeant, round up as many of the council members as you can. Julie, you go along with him and get whoever will come with you to join us at the bank. We need more drivers!"

Julie nodded and raced down the hall behind the sergeant, pulling her coat along with her as she stepped into the street. They took opposite sides of the street and worked their way down the storefronts, calling out to those inside as they went.

By one o'clock, a nice crowd had gathered at the bank.

Outside the skies had turned overcast, and the wind had picked up. A storm was moving in from the northwest, and Julie was thankful that she wouldn't be required to mush out in the blizzard.

"If I may have your attention," Dr. Welch announced. "I have received word from the governor. He has requested we arrange for more relay points along the mail route. The weather forecast has the interior of Alaska turning into a dangerous situation. The suggestion is that more men can travel fewer miles and the risk to life would be reduced significantly."

"But Seppala's already on his way," M. L. Summers declared.

"Yes, I know. He'll no doubt catch up to the serum at one point or another, but instead of having to turn right around and travel all the way back to Nome, he'll only have to make a portion of the journey. I need volunteers to go out along the lines of the mail route and position themselves at the roadhouses."

Several hands went up, including Sam's. Julie caught her breath. What if the storm grew so bad that Sam's life was threatened? Could she stand to see him go, risking his life and the possibility of never returning, without declaring her love?

Her love? Julie tested the thought again. *Yes,* she thought excitedly. *I do love him. I really do, and to lose him now would be devastating.* She didn't hear the rest of Dr. Welch's speech. Her mind was intent on how she could share her heart with Sam. She couldn't throw herself into his arms and tell him, or could she?

The meeting broke up, and Julie recognized Gunnar Kaasen and Ed Rohn as they had both agreed, with Sam, to participate on the serum run. She waited nervously for Dr. Welch to finish instructing the three men so that she could talk to Sam.

After several minutes, Julie thought better of talking to Sam in public and made her way down the hall. There hadn't been all that much snow, she reasoned, so she'd walk to Sam's house on the edge of Nome and wait for him there.

Julie was grateful to see that the storm was skirting to the east of Nome. It was headed directly toward the path the serum would have to take, so Julie prayed that it would pass quickly and blow itself out into Norton Sound before it could cause harm to the dog teams. She hurried to Sam's house and went inside to wait for him.

Minutes later, Sam arrived. He was busy with the dogs outside the back door, but Julie knew he'd have to come inside to get provisions before leaving. Nervously, she twisted her hands, wondering what to say when he finally appeared.

Outside, the wind howled, and while it hadn't yet begun to snow, Sam recognized the dangerous look of the storm. He quickly harnessed his best dogs to the sled, deciding to take eight strong malamutes, then made his way into the house.

Julie almost laughed at the shocked expression on Sam's face as he came rushing through the back door, nearly knocking her to the floor.

"Oh, Sam," Julie said as her voice cracked. She was quite frightened for him and threw herself into his arms, just as she'd thought she couldn't do.

"What's all this about?" Sam questioned as he pulled away just enough to see Julie's face.

"I'm so frightened for you, and I just couldn't let you go out there without telling you...." Julie's words faded as she lowered her head.

Sam lifted her face to meet his gaze. "Telling me what?"

"That I love you," Julie said and broke into tears. "Oh, Sam, I love you so much it hurts."

Sam laughed out loud and whirled Julie in a circle. Julie sobbed all the harder as she thought of how she'd come to love Sam's boisterous laugh and wondered if, after today, she'd ever hear it again.

"Now stop that," Sam said as he held Julie's trembling body against his own. Her tears pained him in a way he'd never known. "Don't cry, Julie. Everything is going to be all right. You'll see."

"But the storm is coming up too fast, and you have to go so far to get to your point on the relay. I couldn't bear it if I lost you now," she cried.

"Nothing's going to happen to me, silly. I've got too much to live for now that I have you. Did you really mean it? Do you honestly love me?"

Julie rolled her still-damp eyes. "How can you ask that? I thought you knew I loved you before I knew."

"Then everything is going to work out. God sent you to me, and He won't separate us now," Sam said confidently.

"Can we pray?" Julie asked as she wiped at her tears with the back of her hand. "I mean, together?"

"Oh, Julie," Sam's face sobered as he spoke, "I'd love to pray with you. Come on." He led the way to the front room where Julie had previously fallen asleep. He stopped and knelt in front of the small table that held his Bible. "Come here," he motioned, and Julie felt a sudden peace.

Kneeling beside him, Julie felt Sam take hold o her hand in his. With his free hand, Sam began to turn the pages of the Bible. Julie reached up and stopped him.

"May I?" she asked with huge, saucer eyes.

"Of course," Sam replied and let Julie turn to Psalm 121.

"'I will lift up mine eyes unto the hills,'" Julie read, "'from whence cometh my help. My help cometh from the Lord, which made heaven and earth. He will not suffer thy foot to be moved: he that keepeth thee will not slumber. Behold, he that keepeth Israel shall neither slumber nor sleep.'"

She paused for a moment, then lifted her gaze from the Bible and recited the words while looking into Sam's dark eyes. "'The Lord is thy keeper: the Lord is thy shade upon thy right hand. The sun shall not smite thee by day, nor the moon by night. The Lord shall preserve thee from all evil: he shall preserve thy soul. The Lord shall preserve thy going out and thy coming in from this time forth, and even for evermore.'"

"Amen," Sam replied when Julie had finished.

"Amen," Julie echoed. "I feel much better giving you over to the Lord than just worrying about you and struggling through it alone."

Sam helped Julie to her feet and kissed her gently on the lips. "I love you, Julie. You've made me a very happy man today, and when I get back and this epidemic is behind us, I'll expect an answer to my proposal."

Julie nodded and after one last hug, she rushed from the room and hurried back to work.

By five-thirty, Dr. Welch was sending an exhausted Julie back to the hospital to rest. She had taken to sleeping in the same room she'd occupied her first night in Nome, and after being up and working for over twelve hours, Julie was ready to relax.

Julie made her way through the deserted streets, wondering about the serum that would save the lives of many and whether Sam was safely to his destination. She paid little attention to anything else, until a whining sound at her feet brought Julie's full attention to the source.

"Kodiak!" she exclaimed as she reached down to the dog's obviously cut harness. She felt her heart skip a beat as she recognized blood on Kodiak's fur. Pulling him into better light, Julie could see that he'd been injured.

Scooping the dog into her arms, Julie made her way

to the hospital. Mindless of Nurse Emily's protests, Julie took Kodiak to her room and flipped on the lights.

"What happened to you, boy?" Julie asked as she examined the dog. He was suffering from cuts on his face and neck, but otherwise looked to be in decent shape. But if Kodiak had been cut loose from the harness, Sam was in trouble.

Bedding the dog down in her room, Julie pulled the pins from her nurse's cap and tossed it to the table. She slipped out of her uniform and donned heavy wool long johns and denim jeans before pulling on reliable seal-skin pants.

She tucked a heavy flannel shirt into her pants and pulled on thick wool socks and her mukluks. Throwing together a bag of supplies, including her medical bag, Julie gave Kodiak her promise to find Sam, locked the door behind her, and went to harness her dog team.

Julie searched unsuccessfully for someone who might help her. She caught up with Dr. Welch at one of the quarantine homes and begged for his help.

"I can't leave Nome, Julie. You know these people are dying," Dr. Welch said firmly. "Try to find someone else to help you. If Sam is hurt, bring him to the hospital, and then I can better serve him."

"I understand," Julie said in a resigned tone. She went in search of anyone who might accompany her, and when no one offered to help, Julie made the decision to go alone.

She packed extra ropes and blankets on her sled,

uncertain of what she might need or how far she'd have to go to find Sam. Against her better judgment, Julie retrieved Kodiak from her room.

"I'm sorry, boy," she said as she brought the dog out into the sub-zero darkness. "I need you to help me find Sam." Kodiak yipped as if he understood and paced back and forth until Julie finished hanging two lighted lanterns from her sled.

She had planned on harnessing Kodiak to her own team, but realized he would be of more help if she allowed him to run free. "All right, boy," she called out to Kodiak. "find Sam."

She mushed the team out behind Kodiak and was surprised to find that the wounded dog responded as though he were in perfect condition. "Dear God," Julie breathed as the wind assaulted her face, "please help me find Sam, and please let him be alive and safe."

Cold numbed Julie's face as she struggled to fix her parka hood. How far would she have to go in order to find Sam? Should she take the time to get her brother and father's help? As Kodiak picked up the pace, Julie decided against any detours. A delay could mean death.

The trail was overblown with snow. Steep, icy embankments lined the Bering side, and darkness made it impossible to see. But Julie was sure of her dogs and pressed on.

After an hour, Kodiak began to yip and slow his pace. Suddenly, the dog howled and danced around. Julie stopped the team and buried the snow hook.

"Sam! Sam!" she called out and listened in the silence for a reply.

Kodiak sat at the side of the embankment and whined. Julie grabbed one of the sled's lanterns and peered over the edge. At the bottom of the embankment rested Sam's overturned sled.

"Sam!"

Julie returned to her sled and pulled out two lengths of rope. She secured them to the sled and threw them down the embankment. She also retrieved several blankets from the sled and tossed them after the ropes. Then taking her medical bag and lantern, she gripped the rope and worked her way down the embankment.

When she reached the bottom of the icy slope, Julie was stunned by what she saw. Several of Sam's dogs were dead. Her heart beat faster as she righted the sled, praying that it wouldn't reveal Sam's dead body. The sled turned over with a thud and exposed nothing more than an indentation in the snow.

"Sam, where are you?" Julie called into the night. The yips of several dogs sent her in search of their source. A few yards away, Julie found the rest of the team faithfully surrounding Sam's lifeless form. He'd been able to cut the dogs loose from the tangled harness before he passed out in the snow.

Julie positioned the lantern to offer the best light and spread a blanket beside Sam. The dogs seemed to know that their job was done, and they allowed Julie to work without interference. She gently rolled Sam onto the blanket.

"Oh, Sam," she whispered as she saw the matted blood in his hair. Examining more closely, Julie found a nasty cut along Sam's hairline. She felt quickly for a pulse to assure herself that he was still alive.

Finding a steady pulse and realizing that the bleeding was minimal, Julie wasted no time tending the wound except to wrap it with a length of bandage. She examined Sam's sled basket to see if it was in good enough shape to use. The runners and the basket's side were broken, but the damaged sled would work well enough to get Sam up the embankment.

Working the ropes around the sled, Julie prayed for strength. She had to take off her mittens for several minutes at a time in order to tie the ropes securely. Fearing frostbite, she worked quickly to finish with the ropes.

When she felt confident that the sled was secured, Julie positioned the basket beside Sam's still form. Wrapping the blanket around Sam, Julie rolled his body into the basket and tied him securely in place. The dogs who'd survived the accident scurried up the embankment behind Julie as she prepared to pull Sam up.

Realizing Sam's dogs could help, Julie pulled out an extra harness and added them to her team. Then she pulled the snow hook and took hold of the harness.

"Come on, boys. Let's go," she called as she pulled them forward. The dogs strained against the basket, but pulled eagerly as if they sensed the life-and-death issue at hand.

As the basket with Sam's battered body appeared over the top of the embankment, Julie quickly secured the snow hook and went to him. He was still unconscious.

"Please, God," she prayed as she packed Sam in blankets. "Please help me to get him home."

Julie knew the basket containing Sam's body was useless for the trail. Using all her strength, she lifted first one end of the broken basket and then the other until she'd managed to place it solidly atop her own sled. Convinced that Sam was as safe as she could make him, Julie moved the dogs out and headed for Nome.

fourteen

Julie paced anxiously while Dr. Welch inspected Sam's wounds. She tried to remain objective, reminding herself that she could only help if she kept her fears under control.

"There's quite a bit of swelling," Dr. Welch said as he finished his examination of Sam, "especially his left eye. We'll watch him closely. Hand me some gauze, please."

Automatically, Julie performed her duties as she would for anyone else, but her heart kept reminding her that this wasn't just anyone else. This was the man she loved. What would she do if he didn't make it? Julie watched Dr. Welch stitch up Sam's head wound.

"Why doesn't he wake up? He should be awake by now." She knew she sounded frantic.

"Julie, you're a nurse. Get a hold of yourself or leave the room. You know these things, especially when they involve concussions, are very unpredictable."

"I know," Julie replied. "I just wish it didn't have to happen to Sam."

"We've done all we can," Dr. Welch said as he taped

a bandage in place. "Now, we'll have to wait and see what happens. Come along."

Julie nodded and went to the sanctuary of her own room. As soon as she closed the door, she fell to her knees and threw herself against the bed. "Dear God, I love Sam so very much. Please help him." Julie stayed on her knees praying for over an hour. When the clock chimed eleven, she rose and went down the hall to where Sam lay motionless.

Sitting beside his bed, Julie held Sam's hand and felt for a pulse. Finding it steady and strong, she exhaled deeply. She patted Sam's hand gently and spoke to him as if he were wide awake.

"Sam, I wanted you to know that your dogs have been cared for. I treated them as if they were my own. Kodiak had some nasty cuts, but I washed them out and put salve on them. He'll be just fine. I knew you'd be worried about the dogs, so I wanted to tell you." She grimaced as she leaned closer. Sam's left eye looked painfully swollen, and Julie offered up a prayer for his healing.

"I love you, Sam. Please wake up. Please be all right," she whispered as she held his hand against her face.

Julie sat in the soft light and watched Sam's chest rise and fall in even, rhythmic breathing. She lost track of time, needing to know that Sam was alive, even if he wasn't conscious.

"Julie?"

Julie roused herself, startled to find that she'd fallen asleep.

"Julie?" The strained, husky voice belonged to Sam.

"Oh, Sam!" Julie said with tears streaming down her face. "You're awake. Oh, thank God."

"Where am I?" he asked weakly.

"The Nome hospital," Julie answered and rinsed out a cloth in cool water. She placed it against Sam's forehead.

"I hurt," Sam said with a sheepish grin. "I guess I took a bit of a fall."

"Just a bit." Julie returned the smile.

"Who brought me in?"

"I did," Julie answered and nearly laughed at the surprised look that crossed Sam's face. "I tried to get someone to help me, but with the epidemic and the serum run, well, people were just preoccupied."

"How did you find me?" Sam asked as he tried painfully to sit up.

"Stay put," Julie said with firm hands upon Sam's shoulders. "You took a nasty hit on the head, and you need to rest."

Sam fell weakly back against the pillows. "All right."

"Kodiak found me," Julie said abruptly.

"Kodiak? Is he okay?"

"He's fine. He's cut up a bit, but he led me to you and helped to pull us back to Nome."

"What about the others?"

"There were four dead when I got there," Julie said softly. "I'm sorry, Sam. I know how you love your dogs."

"I remember cutting them loose from the harness, but after that—nothing."

"The dogs saved your life," Julie added. "They were keeping you from freezing to death when I found you."

"They're a good bunch," Sam said, sounding tired.

"You'd better rest now. I'll check in on you from time to time, and Dr. Welch will be back in the morning," Julie said and got to her feet to leave.

Sam took hold of her hand and pulled her down. "Kiss me," he said, refusing to let go of her.

"Same old Sam," Julie said and pressed her lips gently against his.

Sam smiled up at Julie. "You wouldn't have me any other way," he murmured.

"No," Julie said, "I suppose I wouldn't." She gently let go of Sam's hand. "Now, sleep."

Julie divided her time between Sam and the diphtheria patients. She was glad to see Sam's body healing so quickly, but worried as he became more moody and distant.

"I've brought you a special lunch," Julie said as she brought Sam a tray she'd prepared for him.

"I don't want it," Sam said and continued reading the newspaper that she'd brought him that morning.

"Sam," Julie said as she put the tray on the table beside his bed, "why are you doing this to me?"

"What do you mean?"

"Do you still love me?" Julie asked directly.

Sam's grim expression softened a bit. "This has nothing to do with you. Of course I still love you."

"Then what is this all about? Why are you so angry?" Julie demanded. "It's more than enough that I deal with dying children day by day. It's almost too much to bear that with all the schooling and training I've received, I still can't help them. Now you're acting strange, and I haven't a clue what it's all about."

"This," Sam said as he threw the paper down, "is what it's all about."

Julie noticed the headlines. They were bold reminders that the life-saving serum was ever closer to Nome. "I don't understand. You're upset because the serum run is nearly complete?"

"I don't expect you to understand," Sam said and folded his arms across his chest. "It's just that I wanted to be part of it. I wanted to help bring the serum to Nome. Instead I'm here in this hospital like a useless lump of coal."

"Sam Curtiss, I don't believe you. You were nearly killed, and now you're feeling sorry for yourself?"

"I told you I didn't expect you to understand. Now just let me alone. I'll deal with it myself."

"I will not," Julie said firmly. "Would you walk away from me, if I were behaving this way?"

Sam grinned sheepishly. "You have acted this way and, no, I didn't leave you alone."

"Well, then," Julie said and pulled a chair up to Sam's bedside, "I'm just as stubborn as you are and," she paused and smiled lovingly, "I care just as much."

Sam shook his head. "I've always been lucky, fortunate, blessed, whatever people want to call it. I usually get what I set my mind on, and it's hard not to go on getting my way."

"I'm certain that for a man like you, missing out on something important is very difficult, but God has all of this in His perfect plan. Sam, it doesn't matter that you won't be the one to bring the serum into Nome. What matters is that the serum gets here safely without any more loss of life."

"I know all that. Believe me, I've reasoned it out in my head, but I wanted to do this. Not just for me, mind you." Sam paused and seemed to struggle to put his feelings into words. "But for God. He's done so much for me, and I wanted to offer Him a small token of thanks."

"You do many things that offer God thanks, Sam. You are a positive asset to God's family, and you simply need to keep in mind that whatever you do, you are doing the work of God."

"Colossians 3:23, uh?" Sam said reluctantly.

"'And whatsoever ye do, do it heartily, as to the Lord, and not unto men,'" Julie quoted. "My mother was fond of that verse. She told me that anything a person did was a mission for God so long as they committed their ways to Him."

"Kind of humbles a guy," Sam said with a grin.

"It doesn't matter that you didn't run the serum, Sam. It doesn't matter what you do, so long as you do it for God and do it for His glory. I'd love you whether you raised dogs or panned gold. It doesn't matter to me what you do with your life so long as it's committed to God's will and I'm part of it," Julie said with all her heart.

Sam wrapped his arms around Julie. "You will always be a part of my life," he whispered against her ear. "Just as God will always be at the center of it. I'm glad you had the strength of faith to speak directly with me. We're going to be good for each other, because when one of us falls, the other will lift him up."

"Two are better than one," Julie murmured.

"Yes," Sam said. "Reminds me of Genesis 2:18: 'And the Lord God said, It is not good that the man should be alone; I will make him an help meet for him.' Will you be that for me, Julie? Will you marry me?"

Julie held up her left hand. "You told me one day I'd come to you wearing this ring and you would have your answer. Well, here I am, and the answer is yes."

fifteen

Sam was released from the hospital the next day. The first thing he did was to find a minister who could leave the sick and dying long enough to perform a wedding ceremony.

Julie was heading from the hospital to the doctor's office when Sam caught up with her. Protesting all the way, Julie allowed Sam to lead her to the church.

"But, Sam," she said as they neared the church building, "I'm still wearing my nurse's uniform."

"It doesn't matter," Sam said with a grin. "You could be wearing long johns and it wouldn't matter to me. Besides, it's white."

Julie sighed and realized the weariness that threatened to overtake her. "I suppose you're right. It's just that, well," she paused as they approached the church steps. "A girl kind of has in mind all of her life the type of wedding she wants. This just doesn't fit my dream."

Sam stopped and pulled Julie into his arms. "Look," he said softly, "if you don't want to get married today, I understand. I won't force this on you."

Julie looked up at Sam, noticing the bandage on his

forehead and the discoloration around his eye. He was still handsome to her and with all of her heart she wanted to be his wife. "No one's forcing anything on me," Julie answered as she reached up and pushed a wave of brown hair back off Sam's face. "I want to marry you today."

"Maybe we could have a big church wedding after the epidemic is resolved. I heard that the serum is due in within twenty-four hours, that is if the weather holds."

"That would be wonderful," Julie said to both thoughts.

"Well then, let's not keep the minister waiting," Sam said and pulled Julie with him up the steps.

It wasn't an ideal wedding, but it was more than enough to serve the purpose for which it was intended. Two people pledged to God and one another that they would love each other forever and never allow anything or anyone to come between them.

Looking down at the ring on her finger later that day, Julie remembered the hasty ceremony. She tried to imagine how surprised her father and brother would be when they received the short letter she'd sent. With the quarantine in place and no telephone at the Eriksson household, it was difficult to get information to them.

Her father would be pleased; August, too. Of that, Julie was certain. How she wished they could have given her away to Sam. For a fleeting moment, Julie thought of her mother. Agneta would have approved of the hurried wedding.

Julie's reflections were pushed aside, however, in the face of Nome's crisis. Once again she'd been called to the house of yet another victim of diphtheria, and as she felt the forehead of a small Eskimo girl, Julie's happy memories blurred. The child was burning with fever and most likely would die sometime soon. It seemed strange that something as wonderful as her wedding day would also be the day this child's parents would bury their only daughter.

Julie moved from one house to another. Always, she found various stages of diphtheria. Many were frightened at the news that they were showing the early signs of the disease. Julie worked to calm their nerves, reminding each one that the serum was due into Nome any day. Others were too sick to worry, and Julie prayed aloud for them as she nursed their weakened bodies.

As Julie stood beside the cradle of an eight-month-old baby, she thought how unjust it all was. There was help for this disease. She had training and skills that should save lives, but it still wasn't enough.

"God," she whispered, "why must it be this way?" She thought of the verses in Job and of her mother's dying. Surely her father had voiced that question enough times while sitting beside his dying wife. Hadn't Julie herself asked it of God? She remembered how her mother had correlated verses in Job with everyday life.

"Julie, we don't always know why God allows certain things to happen. We can't have all the answers just yet, because God knows they would be too much for our human minds to comprehend," her mother had told her. "God, in His sovereign wisdom, made all things for a purpose, and how each of those things comes into this world or goes out is entirely up to Him."

"'Whence then cometh wisdom? and where is the place of understanding?'" Julie's mother had shared from Job 28:20. Julie remembered the moment with fondness. Her mother's greatest desire had been for her family to understand that her illness was neither just nor unjust. It was part of God's overall picture for their lives. That same chapter had answered its questions: "And unto man he said, Behold, the fear of the Lord, that is wisdom; and to depart from evil is understanding."

Julie lifted the dying infant into her arms. The baby's lifeless eyes stared up at her as his tiny lungs drew a final breath. She felt the child's body shudder and knew that he was gone. Gone from this earth but at peace in heaven with his Creator. Julie noted the time, returned the infant to his cradle, and recorded facts about the death before breaking the news to the parents.

Several hours later, Dr. Welch found Julie in a near stupor as she sat beside a child while its mother napped.

"You need to get some rest," Dr. Welch said as he checked the child over. "You've been on duty for over twelve hours by my calculations, and that's too much. Go home, Julie. Go home and get some rest."

"I'm fine," Julie said as she stood on the opposite side of the child's bed. "This is Joey. He's only been showing signs of diphtheria for the last eight hours. Temperature is 101 degrees, and his throat is sore, but not overwhelmingly so."

"Good," Dr. Welch said as he finished listening to the boy's chest. "The serum should arrive in time to fix you right up, son." The boy smiled weakly, but didn't say anything. He'd already told Julie it hurt to talk, and she had encouraged him to remain silent.

Dr. Welch packed his bag and headed for the open bedroom door. "Don't tarry any longer than you have to, Julie. Go home and sleep."

Julie nodded, even though she had no intention of obeying.

When Dr. Welch returned to his office, he picked up the telephone and put a call through to Sam.

"Sam?" he said as a voice sounded through the line.

"Yes, this is Sam Curtiss."

"Sam, this is Dr. Welch. Look, I need you to come get your wife."

"Is she sick?" Panic filled Sam's heart.

"No, but she will be if she doesn't get some rest. She's ready to collapse, and I've tried to send her home to sleep, but she won't go. I was hoping you could come force the issue."

"No problem. I'll be right there," Sam answered. "By the way, where should I look for her?"

"I left her at the Davis house. I imagine she'll be there for a while."

"I'm on my way," Sam said and hung up the phone. *Stubborn woman,* he thought as he pulled on his coat and hiked out into the darkened streets.

At the Davis house, Sam knocked, then opened the door and walked in. Mrs. Davis appeared in the hallway just as Sam stepped inside. "Sam Curtiss," she said in a surprised tone. "What are you doing here?"

"I've come to get my wife," Sam said firmly. "I'm sorry to bother you, but the doc says she needs to rest and won't go home."

The woman nodded and led Sam to her son's bedroom. "She's in there," Mrs. Davis said as she opened the door. "I tried to get her to take a break, but she wouldn't hear it."

Sam looked in to find Julie's dozing form as she sat beside the sleeping boy. Gently, Sam helped her to her feet and led her from the room.

"Sam," Julie protested. "What are you doing here?"

"Doc sent me," Sam said as he took Julie's parka from Mrs. Davis. "He said you were to go home and sleep and that he didn't want to see you back until you were rested."

"But—"

"No buts," Sam said, helping her into her coat. "You're going home if I have to carry you—and you know that's no idle threat—so just be cooperative and we won't cause a scene."

"These people need me," Julie said as the parka fell into place. "I can't leave them."

"You aren't any good to them if you're dead on your feet."

"You don't understand the importance of what I do," Julie said as Sam led her out into the street.

"You're in our prayers, Mrs. Davis," Sam said as he pulled Julie along. The woman waved from her door. "Now listen to me," he continued with Julie, "no job is worth killing yourself over. You have an important duty to these people, but it's certainly not one that anyone expects you to die doing."

Julie tried to jerk away from Sam's grip. Maybe marrying Sam had been a mistake. Maybe he was going to expect her to give up her nursing career. Her mind reeled as Sam forced her along. They hadn't consummated their marriage, Julie reasoned. Perhaps she could dissolve it. But that wasn't what she wanted, either. Besides, she loved Sam, and she had made a promise to God to continue loving and obeying him. If Sam told her to quit nursing, she would have to go along.

Just then, George Maynard came rushing down the

street.

"It's the serum," he yelled. "The governor's relayed for us to halt the run because of the weather. Gunnar Kaasen will have to lay over in Solomon until the storm clears."

"He can't," Julie said as she felt her strength give way. "He can't!"

"Hush, Julie," Sam said as he pulled her close. "George, are you sure there's no way to get the drivers through?"

"The wind is blowing up to forty knots, and that coupled with the snow is making it impossible for anyone to get through."

"But people are dying," Julie said nearing hysteria. "They have to get the serum through. They have to."

Sam steadied Julie's trembling body. "Look, keep us posted. I need to get my wife home for some rest."

"Your wife?" George questioned in surprise.

Sam grinned. "Yeah, we were married in between jobs."

"Well, congratulations! It's nice that something decent can take place in the middle of this tragedy." George went hurrying off, and Sam helped Julie make it to their house.

By the time they'd reached the house, Julie was sobbing. She'd tried so hard to hold everything inside, but with the fear that the serum wouldn't arrive in time, Julie could no longer control her emotions.

Sam guided her into the house and helped her out of the parka. He could hardly bear the sounds of her sobs, and after pulling his own coat off, he took her into his arms and held her.

"They're going to die without the serum," Julie cried. "I can't bear to watch any more of them die."

"I know. I know," Sam said as he reached up and pulled the pins out of Julie's hair. The ebony mane fell soft across her shoulders, and Sam relished the feel of it.

"I can't help them, Sam," she said looking up with dark, wet eyes. "I'm useless to them."

"Nonsense," Sam said. "Come on. I'm going to take you upstairs and put you to bed. You're tired and distraught with what you've had to deal with today. I wish I could have given you a better wedding day."

Julie allowed Sam to lead her to what was to become their bedroom. Neither she nor Sam were thinking about the romance of their wedding night, however. His only concern was to calm her down and see to it that she got some much-needed sleep.

Julie steadied her nerves and dried her eyes. She was too tired to expend more energy on useless tears. Sam helped her to the edge of the bed, where he knelt down and unlaced her mukluks.

"Now," Sam said as he threw the boots to one side. "You rest, and I'll go get a wet rag for you to wipe your face with."

"No!" Julie exclaimed. "Please don't leave me, Sam. I can't be alone right now."

Sam smiled and unlaced his own boots. "I'll hold you until you're asleep, and even after that, if you like."

"I like," Julie said and moved over to make room for her husband.

Sam eased his weight onto the bed and pulled Julie into his arms. Neither one of them had ever experienced a closeness like this. It was so intimate, so pure.

"Sam," Julie murmured as she put her head upon his chest. "The serum has to get through. We should pray for a miracle."

"You're right, of course. Why didn't we think of that earlier?"

"I don't know. I guess we were just too busy trying to take care of everything ourselves. At least I know I was. I hate myself for always resorting to prayer as a final option," Julie replied.

"Don't hate yourself," Sam stated firmly. "You are a creation of God, and He loves you. I forget the importance of prayer, myself. We'll just pray for a miracle and ask God to deliver the serum into Dr. Welch's hands in record time."

"But if the governor has ordered the race stopped," Julie began, "it would be against the law to continue. Wouldn't it?"

"I suppose it might be perceived that way," Sam said with a nod. "However, a guy has to get the message in order to heed it, right? Maybe Gunnar won't get the message."

"I suppose that's always possible," Julie said with renewed hope. "Thank you for being such an encouragement, Sam."

They prayed together, and Julie fell asleep to the comfort of Sam's powerful, heart-felt words. For the first time in many days, she slept soundly with the assurance that God and Sam were at her side to protect her from the pain of the world.

Sam awoke with a start and, forgetting his wife was nestled in his arms, he woke Julie without meaning to.

"What is it, Sam?" Julie asked as she registered the sound of barking dogs.

"I don't know, but the dogs are going crazy. What time is it, anyway?"

Julie glanced at her watch. "Five-thirty," she replied and got to her feet. "Maybe Dr. Welch has come to find me. Maybe things are worse, and he needs my help."

"You aren't going anywhere," Sam said firmly. "You've only had a little over five hours of sleep, and that simply isn't enough. Get back into bed."

Julie felt as though she'd had a week's worth of sleep and stood with her hands planted firmly on her hips. "I will not be treated like a child, Sam Curtiss. I'm your wife, not one of your dogs."

Sam broke into a hearty laugh. "Well, Julie Curtiss," he said trying the name on for size, "my dogs have better sense than you when it comes to taking care of themselves. However, you are right. I'm used to telling, not asking. I'm sorry. Now, would you please get back into bed?"

The dogs had worked themselves into a feverish pitch, and Julie could stand it no longer. "Sam, please find out what's going on. Please."

Sam lost his resolve as he stared into the pleading eyes of his wife. "Oh, all right. But afterwards, you must get some rest."

"Whatever you say, husband."

Sam was gone only a few minutes. When he returned, he tossed Julie her mukluks. "You'd better get these on."

"What is it, Sam?" Julie asked as she hastened to tie her laces.

"Just come with me," Sam said and hurried down the stairs with Julie close behind him. He brought her parka and waited while Julie pulled it over her head.

"Something's very wrong, isn't it?" Julie asked fearfully.

"On the contrary, Julie. On the contrary," Sam said as he opened the front door. "Hurry."

Sam and Julie raced through the darkened streets and Julie knew instinctively that Sam was leading her to the hospital. They rounded the corner. A dog team stood at the front stairs. Julie's heart skipped a beat as she recognized Balto, a big black-and-white husky who was a favorite of Gunnar's.

"Oh, Sam," she breathed against the sub-zero air. "It's Gunnar's sled! The serum is here!"

"Looks like we got that miracle," Sam said with a grin that spread from ear to ear. "Come on. Let's go see if we can help." Julie nodded and followed her husband up the steps. God was so good!

sixteen

Gunnar's arrival had attracted very little attention. It was too early in the morning for most people, and no one thought the serum would come through because of the governor's mandate.

Julie stood by crying tears of joy as Dr. Welch received the cylindrical package and hurried inside to reveal its contents. Sam and Julie joined the party, but their hearts stopped when Dr. Welch announced that the serum was frozen. Everyone waited in pained anticipation, wondering if the trip had been for nothing. Finally word came from Seattle that the serum would be unharmed from the freezing and simply required a slow warming to bring it back to its original state.

Gunnar Kaasen and his huskies had covered the last fifty-three miles in less than seven-and-a-half hours. The entire serum run had covered more than 674 miles in a record 127.5 hours, bringing with it the renewed hope of life.

By February 21, Nome's quarantine was lifted. It had been exactly one month since the outbreak of the epidemic.

With every passing day, life seemed to take on a more normal routine. Schools reopened, much to the disappointment of the children and the relief of the parents. Store owners were happy to have full shops again, and everywhere people were glad to have lived through the crisis. George Nakoota even showed up to reveal a perfectly healed arm to Dr. Welch.

It was no different at the Curtiss house. Julie and Sam had settled into a comfortable life at the edge of town, and although Julie had been extremely busy nursing the sick and helping Dr. Welch, Sam had been patient with her absences. Julie wondered, however, how long it would be before Sam's patience wore thin and he would demanded that she stay home more.

Several days after the quarantine had been lifted, Julie contemplated the situation as she prepared breakfast. Her heart belonged to Sam, yet part of her belonged to nursing as well.

"You're mighty deep in thought," Sam said as he came into the room and took a seat at the table. He threw the *Nome Nugget* on the chair beside him and smiled. "I suppose you're thinking about the serum run again."

"Well, as a matter of fact, I heard something quite fascinating yesterday," Julie said as she offered Sam a plate of fried eggs and bacon. She returned to the counter where she retrieved a stack of freshly baked biscuits. Their tantalizing aroma filled the air, and as soon as Julie placed them on the table, Sam reached for one.

"No doubt another miracle," Sam teased. Julie had been enthralled by the stories of miraculous blessings that enabled the drivers to deliver the diphtheria anti-toxin to Nome in only five-and-a-half days.

Julie put her own plate of food on the table and joined Sam. "You know how I love the way God moved in this crisis," she smiled. "I just can't help being fascinated with it."

"I know, Julie, and I feel the same way. Let's have a prayer." Sam took her hands. "Father, we thank You for the bounty of our table and for the healing of our community. We praise You that the deaths were few and that the medicine was provided in a much quicker time than any of us dreamed possible. Amen."

Sam started eating as Julie began to tell what she'd heard. "Leonhard Seppala cut out a lot of distance by taking a short cut across Norton Sound. The water was frozen solid, but it was difficult for him to see his way so he had to rely upon the dogs."

"I'd heard that," Sam answered. "It takes a brave man to venture out across an open bay like that. Even if it is frozen solid at the shores, you can't know how it will be once you get out in the middle of the inlet."

"Well, as wondrous as that was, what happened after Leonhard crossed the sound gives even more cause for praise," Julie said, leaning forward. "Not more than three-and-a-half hours after Leonhard crossed Norton Sound, the entire thing broke up, and the ice moved out into the Bering Sea. The crossing would have taken Leonhard's life, no doubt, had he attempted it at a later time. Talk about the hand of God!"

"Incredible," Sam said as he paused between bites. "Our God is truly a God of miracles."

"Leonhard's shortcut saved hours and probably many lives, Sam. I'm amazed that he was able to stay on the sled. After all, he'd mushed those dogs for more than 169 miles just to get to the serum at Shaktolik. Then to turn around and travel another ninety-one miles to get the serum closer to Nome, well. . . ." Julie shook her head. "It staggers my imagination."

"That lead dog of his is something else," Sam said, sipping his coffee. "His name is Togo, and Leonhard never thought he'd amount to much—that is until he jumped the fence one day and followed Leonhard across part of the interior. Leonhard finally harnessed him up to keep him out of trouble. Lo and behold, the dog's a born leader!"

"Thanks to Togo and the other dogs, Nome is safe, and the epidemic has been defeated," Julie said. "I simply can't imagine the way God planned this all out. Who can know the mind of God?"

"I know how much you've enjoyed learning about the

hazards that the men met on the trail. I have one that I think you will find quite rewarding," Sam said with a smile.

"Oh, tell me Sam! What did you hear?" Julie asked as she leaned forward, her eyes wide in anticipation.

"You remember we heard that the run was to be halted because of the weather?"

"Sure, I do," Julie said with a nod. "How could I forget? I've never lost control like that in my life."

"Well," Sam continued, "it was just about the time we decided to pray that Gunnar Kaasen made the decision to drive on past Solomon and keep the serum moving. He felt compelled to go on and not waste time with a stop. No one had the opportunity to tell him about the mandate from the governor because he never stopped."

"It's just like you said," Julie remembered. "A man can't be faulted for not doing what he knows nothing about. Good for Gunnar!"

"Well, there's more," Sam said as he finished his breakfast. "The wind came up something fierce, and Gunnar couldn't see a thing in front of him. All of a sudden his lead dog, Balto, stopped dead in his tracks. Gunnar couldn't understand why, but Balto wouldn't budge."

"What happened?" Julie asked, captivated by Sam's story.

"Balto had led the team out across the Topkok River,

and it wasn't solidly frozen. Balto was standing in running water when he came to a stop."

"Poor thing," Julie sympathized. "His feet could have frozen to the ice. What did Gunnar do? Balto looked just fine when they got into Nome."

"Gunnar's a good man. He thought fast and unharnessed Balto. There was plenty of powdered snow on the banks, so Gunnar rubbed Balto's feet in it until they were fairly dry."

"How ingenious! I've got to remember that one when I'm out on my route," Julie said, braving a reference to her job. Even though the epidemic was over, Julie hadn't found the nerve to talk with Sam about her nursing career. She started to clear the table to avoid Sam's reaction.

"It never hurts to be prepared, and the more you know about surviving accidents, the better off you are. That's what made me so mad about my own accident," Sam reflected. "I knew better than to take the risks I was taking. I should have slowed down a bit and paid more attention. However," he added with a grin, "there was a certain black-haired nurse on my mind. It seems she had just told me that she loved me." Sam pushed his chair back and pulled Julie onto his lap.

"Oh, Sam," Julie whispered against his hair. How she wished she could clear things up and explain how she felt about her work. She was so afraid that if she insisted on continuing her nursing career, Sam would stop loving her.

Sam nuzzled his lips against Julie's neck and began kissing her. Julie found the contact electrifying, yet she knew she needed to finish getting ready for work. As gently as she could, she pushed Sam away.

"I've got to finish up here and get down to the hospital," she said and jumped up abruptly. Sam's surprised face told it all. "I'm sorry," Julie whispered and hurried to wash the breakfast dishes.

Sam's silence worried Julie. She wiped the soap suds from her hands and went back to the table where he was still sitting.

"We should talk," she said and waited for Sam to put down the newspaper.

"What about?" Sam asked hesitantly. Julie hadn't been her normal self the last few days, and he wasn't sure that he was up to dealing with whatever was troubling her.

"Sam, do you know how long I dreamed of becoming a nurse?"

"I know it was a long-time dream. I know, too, that it was a dream you shared with your mother."

"Yes, that's right," Julie said, searching her mind for the right words. "Being a nurse is very important to me, not just because it's a job I do every day, but because of the need. These people are without many of the comforts available in the States, and I want to be a part of seeing to it that they have what they need in the way of health care."

"It's an admirable position," Sam said as he reached out for Julie. "I've always admired your determination and dedication."

Julie stepped back to avoid Sam's touch. He frowned but said nothing.

"It's my determination and dedication to what I believe God wants me to do," Julie said stressing the reference to God. She paused to see what Sam's reaction might be. His face was unreadable.

"Go on," he said unemotionally. He was troubled by the way Julie had distanced herself from his touch. She hadn't seemed herself since the critical part of the epidemic had passed. Sam was determined to get to the bottom of whatever was bothering her.

"I love what I do, Sam. I love to help people, and I enjoy my work with the natives."

"I don't see what you're getting at Julie," Sam said more impatiently than he'd intended. "I know that you love your job. I know you love the people and the land. What I don't know is what this has to do with us and why you're acting so strangely."

Sam got up and took two long strides to where Julie stood. He reached out to hold her, but Julie turned away.

"Please don't touch me. I'm trying to explain this to

you, and you aren't making matters any easier," Julie said, close to tears.

"Julie, are you sorry that you married me?"

Julie turned back quickly and shook her head. "No, Sam. I love you, and I hope that you still love me."

"Of course I love you." Sam could no longer stand Julie's coolness. He took her into his arms and crushed her to his chest. "I will always love you," he whispered as his lips pressed a long, passionate kiss upon hers.

Julie melted against Sam. She could never imagine life without him. Maybe giving up her career was the only way she could save her marriage. Tears streamed from her eyes. A sob escaped her throat, causing Sam to pull back.

"What in the world?" he muttered and dropped his hands. "I don't understand what this is all about, but I've had just about enough." He stormed out of the room, barely remembering his parka as he went out into the cold.

Julie jumped at the sound of the front door slamming. Knowing it would be impossible to work, Julie retreated upstairs, locked herself in their bedroom, and had a good long cry.

seventeen

Julie lost track of time as she contemplated her misery. How could she explain her heart to Sam without hurting him? She loved him so much, yet she felt torn.

She looked around the room that had been hers for a little over a month. Everything here spoke of Sam; the large walnut dresser, the huge four-poster bed, and even the lamps on the night stands looked masculine and powerful. The room smelled like the heady cologne Sam liked to wear.

"Father," Julie prayed, "I wanted to serve You." Before she could continue, it came to Julie's mind that if she truly wanted to serve God, she'd open her heart and skills to whatever job He gave her. Perhaps the job God wanted Julie to do now involved being a good wife and homemaker. Maybe she was trained as a nurse simply to help during the epidemic.

"I need to understand, Lord. Please teach me what it is I'm to do," Julie begged. "I can't bear to hurt Sam, and I can't bear the way I'm feeling."

Julie reached to the night stand and picked up her Bible. She flipped aimlessly through the pages, wondering what God might show her there. When she reached Ephesians, Julie began to read through the verses. "Teach me, Lord," she prayed. "I came home to serve You, and now I have a husband to serve and work with as well."

Just then, Julie's eyes fell upon Ephesians 5:22: "Wives, submit yourselves unto your own husbands, as unto the Lord. For the husband is the head of the wife, even as Christ is the head of the church: and he is the saviour of the body. Therefore as the church is subject unto Christ, so let the wives be to their own husbands in everything." It seemed a clear answer.

"All right, Father," Julie said in earnest, "I trust You to guide me. Sam loves You and seeks Your guidance, and because of this, I believe, without fear, that You will control this situation."

Julie got up and dried her eyes. What should she do? Sam was out there somewhere, and no doubt he was feeling just as confused and troubled as she was. Julie debated trying to find him but chose to wait until he returned. She was determined to make her concerns clear. If Sam insisted she give up nursing, then she'd trust God to give her the grace to do just that.

Julie didn't have long to wait. Within the hour, she heard Sam stomping around through the rooms downstairs. Julie brushed her hair and made her way to the top of the stairs just as Sam was starting up.

"We should talk," Julie said softly.

Sam nodded. The anger was gone and in his eyes shone the love that Julie had come to count on.

Julie made her way down the stairs and took Sam's extended hand. "I'm sorry for the way I've been acting. I know you deserve a lot better, and I feel bad about it."

"If I've done something wrong, you should tell me," Sam said as he led Julie to the couch.

"You haven't done anything wrong, Sam. That's what makes this so frustrating to me. I've always been able to speak my mind, but something about you makes me forget myself. I suppose it has a great deal to do with my love for you," Julie said softly. She looked down at her hands, avoiding Sam's face.

"You make your love for me sound like something oppressive," he replied.

"Not oppressive," Julie answered. "Maybe restrictive."

"Restrictive?" Sam questioned. "How so?"

"I'm not sure that restrictive is even the right word. I never expected you to come into my life. I don't know why, but I never considered marrying and having a family. At least not until much later in my life."

"And?"

"And," Julie said with deliberation, "I doubt I would have become a public health nurse if I'd known I would be married so soon into my career."

"I still don't understand," Sam said softly.

Julie looked up at him. "I love my job, but I'm ready to give it up if that's what you tell me to do." There! She'd finally managed to get the words out.

"What in the world are you talking about?" Sam asked, confusion spreading across his face. "Why would I ever ask you to quit nursing?"

"Because it takes me away from you. I have to be on the village routes for most of the year, and those absences would keep us separated for long, long spells. I'm not sure I could bear it myself."

"What makes you think that you'll be separated from me?" Sam asked with a grin. "I know what's required of you on your job. I knew it before I ever married you. I even talked with Dr. Welch at length about it."

"You did?" Julie's surprised voice amused Sam.

"I certainly did. You didn't think I'd walk into something like marriage without knowing exactly what I was doing, did you?"

"I guess I never thought about it," Julie replied. "I was too caught up in the epidemic. What did Dr. Welch tell you?"

"He explained your duties and the schedule you'd be keeping as a public health nurse. He told me you'd go by dog sled in the winter months and horseback in the summer. He also told me that the idea of a woman alone on the trails bothered him. I asked him why someone couldn't accompany you."

"And what did he say?"

"He told me there wasn't funding to support two people on the route. It had been hard enough to get support for one. I told him my idea was to accompany you on the trails without being paid."

"What?" Julie's mouth dropped open. "You'd be willing to go with me?"

"I'd insist. I can't imagine anything more enjoyable than long hours in the wilderness with a beautiful woman who just happens to be my wife. I've had it planned from the beginning."

"I never considered such a thing," Julie said in disbelief. "You'd actually go with me? What a wonderful idea! We wouldn't have to be separated, and you wouldn't want me to quit my job." Julie squealed with delight as she threw herself into Sam's arms.

"Is that what your moodiness has been all about?" Sam asked, holding Julie at arm's length. "Did you think I was going to force you to give up your dream?"

Julie nodded. "I wanted to talk to you about my job before we got married. But then, the epidemic came up, and you nearly got yourself killed, and I just let it go. I was afraid to bring it up after that."

"Never be afraid of me, Julie," Sam said softly. "And please don't ever turn away from me again."

"I'm sorry, Sam, it's just that you being the kind of guy

you are, I thought—"

Sam couldn't resist chuckling as he interrupted. "You mean to tell me you honestly thought I'd expect you to give up something as important as your nursing? I can't believe you'd think so little of me. I mean, I know I can be a little demanding and—"

"A little?" Julie interrupted. "A little?"

Sam shook his head and pulled Julie into his arms. "Okay, so I can be very demanding, but I certainly wouldn't make a decision like that for you. I married you knowing you had a job to do. I admired you for it. I think helping the villages is an important task, and I believe strongly in spreading the Word of God to those who have never heard it before. I kind of figured I might help you."

"Honestly?"

"Honestly," Sam said firmly.

"I'm so sorry for misjudging you," Julie said as she reached a hand up to Sam's bearded face. "I love you so much, and I love my nursing. I didn't want to have to choose between the two."

"I would never have asked you to," Sam said as he kissed Julie tenderly.

Julie felt a burden was lifted from her shoulders. She thought of her willingness to accept whatever Sam had instructed her to do and knew that her peace came in being willing to be obedient to God.

As Sam pulled away from her, she nestled her face against his chest and thanked God for the husband He'd given her. Almost as an afterthought, Julie raised one last question.

"Sam, there are bound to be times when you'll be needed here or when you can't go with me. How will you feel about that?"

"Nothing will keep me from your side," Sam declared.

"But what if something happens and it does? I can't stay home and forget the people in the villages. We should be in agreement what we'll do if that happens," Julie said earnestly.

"If that happens, and I don't believe it will," Sam replied, "then I'll simply wait here with a light in the window until you come home safely to me. Good enough?" Sam's eyes were filled with love.

Julie nodded. She no longer had any doubts about being married to Sam. "I love you, Sam, and I love God for giving me the wisdom to marry you. It will be the light of your love that leads me home and keeps me strong."

"Oh, my beautiful Jewel," Sam said as he leaned back and pulled Julie against him. "That's a light that will never burn out. For as long as I live, it will burn only for you."

epilogue

The 1925 diphtheria epidemic in Nome, Alaska, would have taken more lives and spread farther had it not been for the heroic hearts of the men who mushed the serum run. Their names are listed here in honor of their sacrifice and spirit.

"Wild Bill" Shannon—Nenana to Tolovana (52 miles)
Dan Green—Tolovana to Manley Hot Springs (31 miles)
Johnny Folger—Manley Hot Springs to Fish Lake (28 miles)
Sam Joseph—Fish Lake to Tanana (26 miles)
Titus Nikoli—Tanana to Kallands (34 miles)
Dave Corning—Kallands to Nine Mile mail cabin (24 miles)
Edgar Kalland—Nine Mile to Kokrines (30 miles)
Harry Pitka—Kokrines to Ruby (30 miles)
Bill McCarty—Ruby to Whiskey Creek (28 miles)
Edgar Nollner—Whiskey Creek to Galena (24 miles)
George Nollner—Galena to Bishop Mountain (18 miles)

Charlie Evans—Bishop Mountain to Nulato (30 miles)

Tommy Patsy—Nulato to Kaltag (36 miles)

Jackscrew—Kaltag to Old Woman shelter house (40 miles)

Victor Anagick—Old Woman to Unalakleet (34 miles)

Myles Gonangnan—Unalakleet to Shaktolik (40 miles)

Henry Ivanoff—starts from Shaktolik but meets Seppala

Leonhard Seppala—Shaktolik to Golovin (91 miles)

Charlie Olson—Golovin to Bluff (25 miles)

Gunnar Kaasen—Bluff to Nome (53 miles)

And, of course, the dogs!

My special thanks to the Anchorage Museum of History and Art; Anchorage Municipal Libraries; the University of Alaska, Fairbanks; and my husband Jim for their assistance with the historical research surrounding this event.

A Letter To Our Readers

Dear Reader:

In order that we might better contribute to your reading enjoyment, we would appreciate your taking a few minutes to respond to the following questions. When completed, please return to the following:

Karen Carroll, Editor
Heartsong Presents
P.O. Box 719
Uhrichsville, Ohio 44683

1. Did you enjoy reading *A Light in the Window*?
   ☐ Very much. I would like to see more books
      by this author!
   ☐ Moderately
      I would have enjoyed it more if _____

   _____

2. Are you a member of *Heartsong Presents*? Yes   No
   If no, where did you purchase this book? _____

   _____

3. What influenced your decision to purchase
   this book? (Circle those that apply.)

Cover	Back cover copy
Title	Friends
Publicity	Other _____

4. On a scale from 1 (poor) to 10 (superior), please rate the following elements.

    ___Heroine   ___Plot

    ___Hero   ___Inspirational theme

    ___Setting   ___Secondary characters

5. What settings would you like to see covered in *Heartsong Presents* books?

_____

_____

6. What are some inspirational themes you would like to see treated in future books?_____

_____

_____

7. Would you be interested in reading other *Heartsong Presents* titles?   Yes   No

8. Please circle your age range:

Under 18	18-24	25-34
35-45	46-55	Over 55

9. How many hours per week do you read? _____

Name _____

Occupation _____

Address _____

City _____ State _____ Zip _____

······ Heartsong ······

Great Inspirational Romance at a Great Price!

Heartsong Presents books are inspirational romances in contemporary and historical settings, designed to give you an enjoyable, spirit-lifting reading experience. You can choose from 52 wonderfully written titles from some of today's best authors like Veda Boyd Jones, Linda Herring, Janelle Jamison, and many others.

HEARTSONG PRESENTS TITLES AVAILABLE NOW:

_____HP 1 A TORCH FOR TRINITY, *Colleen L. Reece*
_____HP 2 WILDFLOWER HARVEST, *Colleen L. Reece*
_____HP 3 RESTORE THE JOY, *Sara Mitchell*
_____HP 4 REFLECTIONS OF THE HEART, *Sally Laity*
_____HP 5 THIS TREMBLING CUP, *Marlene Chase*
_____HP 6 THE OTHER SIDE OF SILENCE, *Marlene Chase*
_____HP 7 CANDLESHINE, *Colleen L. Reece*
_____HP 8 DESERT ROSE, *Colleen L. Reece*
_____HP 9 HEARTSTRINGS, *Irene B. Brand*
_____HP10 SONG OF LAUGHTER, *Lauraine Snelling*
_____HP11 RIVER OF FIRE, *Jacquelyn Cook*
_____HP12 COTTONWOOD DREAMS, *Norene Morris*
_____HP13 PASSAGE OF THE HEART, *Kjersti Hoff Baez*
_____HP14 A MATTER OF CHOICE, *Susannah Hayden*
_____HP15 WHISPERS ON THE WIND, *Maryn Langer*
_____HP16 SILENCE IN THE SAGE, *Colleen L. Reece*
_____HP17 LLAMA LADY, *VeraLee Wiggins*
_____HP18 ESCORT HOMEWARD, *Eileen M. Berger*
_____HP19 A PLACE TO BELONG, *Janelle Jamison*
_____HP20 SHORES OF PROMISE, *Kate Blackwell*
_____HP21 GENTLE PERSUASION, *Veda Boyd Jones*
_____HP22 INDY GIRL, *Brenda Bancroft*
_____HP23 GONE WEST, *Kathleen Karr*
_____HP24 WHISPERS IN THE WILDERNESS, *Colleen L. Reece*
_____HP25 REBAR, *Mary Carpenter Reid*
_____HP26 MOUNTAIN HOUSE, *Mary Louise Colln*
_____HP27 BEYOND THE SEARCHING RIVER, *Jacquelyn Cook*
_____HP28 DAKOTA DAWN, *Lauraine Snelling*
_____HP29 FROM THE HEART, *Sara Mitchell*
_____HP30 A LOVE MEANT TO BE, *Brenda Bancroft*

(If ordering from this page, please remember to include it with the order form.)

·········Presents·········

_____HP31 DREAM SPINNER, _Sally Laity_
_____HP32 THE PROMISED LAND, _Kathleen Karr_
_____HP33 SWEET SHELTER, _VeraLee Wiggins_
_____HP34 UNDER A TEXAS SKY, _Veda Boyd Jones_
_____HP35 WHEN COMES THE DAWN, _Brenda Bancroft_
_____HP36 THE SURE PROMISE, _JoAnn A. Grote_
_____HP37 DRUMS OF SHELOMOH, _Yvonne Lehman_
_____HP38 A PLACE TO CALL HOME, _Eileen M. Berger_
_____HP39 RAINBOW HARVEST, _Norene Morris_
_____HP40 PERFECT LOVE, _Janelle Jamison_
_____HP41 FIELDS OF SWEET CONTENT, _Norma Jean Lutz_
_____HP42 SEARCH FOR TOMORROW, _Mary Hawkins_
_____HP43 VEILED JOY, _Colleen L. Reece_
_____HP44 DAKOTA DREAM, _Lauraine Snelling_
_____HP45 DESIGN FOR LOVE, _Janet Gortsema_
_____HP46 THE GOVERNOR'S DAUGHTER, _Veda Boyd Jones_
_____HP47 TENDER JOURNEYS, _Janelle Jamison_
_____HP48 SHORES OF DELIVERANCE, _Kate Blackwell_
_____HP49 YESTERDAY'S TOMORROWS, _Linda Herring_
_____HP50 DANCE IN THE DISTANCE, _Kjersti Hoff Baez_
_____HP51 THE UNFOLDING HEART, _JoAnn A. Grote_
_____HP52 TAPESTRY OF TAMAR, _Colleen L. Reece_
_____HP53 MIDNIGHT MUSIC, _Janelle Burnham_
_____HP54 HOME TO HER HEART, _Lena Nelson Dooley_
_____HP55 TREASURE OF THE HEART, _JoAnn A. Grote_
_____HP56 A LIGHT IN THE WINDOW, _Janelle Jamison_
_____ 58 Free to Love
      59

ABOVE TITLES ARE $2.95 EACH

SEND TO: Heartsong Presents Reader's Service
P.O. Box 719, Uhrichsville, Ohio 44683

Please send me the items checked above. I am enclosing $_____
(please add $1.00 to cover postage per order. OH add 6.5% tax. PA and
NJ add 6%.). Send check or money order, no cash or C.O.D.s, please.
   To place a credit card order, call 1-800-847-8270.

NAME _____

ADDRESS _____

CITY/STATE _____ ZIP_____